STING OF THE BLUE SCORPION
THE ADVENTURES OF PETER
THE BRAZEN, VOLUME 6

STING OF THE
BLUE SCORPION
THE ADVENTURES OF
PETER THE BRAZEN, VOLUME 6

LORING BRENT

ILLUSTRATED BY
SAMUEL CAHAN

COVER BY
PAUL STAHR

POPULAR PUBLICATIONS · 2022

TABLE OF CONTENTS

STING OF THE BLUE SCORPION

*Two people knew the secret lair of Mr. Lu,
the Blue Scorpion of China—and Peter the
Brazen knew they could not betray it and live*

1

THE HAND OF MR. LU

ON HURRYING, STUMBLING feet the girl in the green slicker approached the dimly lighted windows of the Imperial Moon Jade Shop. And behind her, in the fog, she heard the relentless *clip-clop, clip-clop!* of the wooden sandals. They were like the heavy, relentless ticking of some machine of doom.

Once, under a street light with a bleary halo, she saw the man who was wearing the wooden sandals. A short, misshapen man he was, in the scanty garb of a waterfront coolie; a man whose twisted legs and arms gave him, in that terrifying light, the look of a monstrous land crab; a man with but one alert shoe-button of an eye, and the other an empty red socket.

Clip-clop, clip-clop! at her heels. Not more than a couple of hundred feet behind her. Never varying his pace. Always there, scuttling along behind her. *Clip-clop, clip-clop!*

The girl in the green slicker was lost, hopelessly lost. To the dismaying sense of being lost was added the terrifying uncertainty of what that one-eyed follower meant to do. Why was he following her? For what particularly opportune moment was he waiting?

With heart beating high in her breast, the girl in the green slicker pushed on toward the dim lights in the

The apparition muttered a single word: "Death!"

window of the Imperial Moon Jade Shop. She did not know that it was the Imperial Moon Jade Shop. There was nothing on the window but Chinese characters, and she could not read Chinese. But the dim light was a sanctuary. She would go in there and insist that someone go and fetch her a rickshaw.

There were rickshaws, but they were all occupied. One of them occasionally flitted past her, a phantom, with a ghost cuddled under the dripping, shining rubber hood and another ghost padding along with bare feet and bare yellow legs through the black mud.

Clip-clop, clip-clop! The sounds were clear and sharp on flagging. On planking they were muffled and drumlike. They suggested temple drums, sacrifice drums. Even more alarming were the silences when there was no flagging, no planking, when there was nothing but soft mud in which the sandals made no sound. Her ears would seek for it, would hear the soft approaching whisper of an electrify-

ing menace, until she wanted to scream. Then—*clip-clop, clip-clop!* it would suddenly begin again, and send fresh icy shivers along her nerves.

Night had closed down upon Shanghai half an hour ago. With it came the fog, springing up from the swollen brown river like some genie released by the very spirit of darkness. It streamed through the streets in billowing yellow banners. Objects that might have been familiar landmarks were cloaked in tawny mystery. House fronts were vague brown slabs which emanated odors of cookery—boiling fish, boiling weeds. The weeds had been torn out of the shallow water in the river and boiled, then they were eaten, roots and all. A puff of spice drifted down the fog. And there was the smell of sour rice wine.

Figures, huddled into cloaks against the cold clamminess of the fog, flitted past her. Beady eyes slanted at her. And always, back there in the fog, the measured clacking of those wooden sandals: *clip-clop, clip-clop!*

She had been, she assured herself for the hundredth time, a fool to slip away from the cocktail party at the French Consulate merely because Bill Montgomery annoyed her. Yet he had been so damned persistent—so lacking in considerateness! She had wanted to escape that ardent young romantic, and so she had slipped away. But he had followed, and she had darted up the Rue du Consulat to Honan Road, and thence through the North Gate and into the forbidden territory of Chinese City. She had lost Bill Montgomery—and thereupon had lost herself!

Yet the adventure might be said to have its advantages. It had revealed to her that she was being followed. More than that,, it made her suddenly aware that perhaps she had been followed, wherever she went, for heaven only knew how many days. The clacking of those sandals was like a sinister thought which, hiding in some dark recess of her brain, had suddenly pounced on her attention.

Clip-clop, clip-clop!

Hurrying through that dark, twisting, fogbound street, she saw the jade shop as a haven. She paused before the window, but she did not go in at once. She wanted to make sure that the interior of the shop looked safe.

The clacking sound behind her stopped. Was that crab-like creature waiting for her to go on, or was he creeping toward her?

Shivering, the girl in the green slicker looked through the misty sheet of glass. She could not see beyond the samples of jade displayed in the window, but she hoped that the proprietor would see her looking at his wares and would light the shop.

Visible specks of moisture drove, swirling, past the

window, pushing on through their own halo there, as if they were on some important, mysterious errand. After watching them for a few seconds, it was as if the window was moving and the fog standing still. The window, with its display of carved jade, was like some strange ship slowly surging through this thin, fantastic medium.

Dimly, the girl saw a dark shadow moving about in the lesser darkness of the shop. At first her eyes saw none of the jade objects in the window. But these gradually took form. There was the inevitable jade amulet with which a Chinese lover expresses the seriousness of his intentions to his beloved. And there was the inevitable little Confucius, a very old and worn-looking specimen, as if he had been carried around in somebody's pocket, bringing wisdom and good fortune.

SUDDENLY, THE GIRL saw the little white jade symbol of the three great Chinese virtues: three monkeys carved from one piece, with the hands of one clapped to his mouth, the hands of another clapped to his eyes, the hands of the third clapped to his ears. "Hear no evil—see no evil—speak no evil!"

The first effect of this carving upon the girl was illusory—as if a black cloud had blossomed forth inside her head.

And her mind harked back to a night, some months ago—to an oblong, sapphire-blue box that had come aboard a little river steamer, a moment before the ship's departure from the filthy, squalid village of Chung-King.

That box had contained the embalmed heads of three red-haired men, and the hands of these three men. The hands of one were nailed down with bronze spikes to his eyes. The hands of another were nailed down with bronze spikes to his ears. While the hands of the third were nailed down with bronze spikes to his mouth.—"Hear no evil—see no evil—speak no evil!"

Susan O'Gilvie had not seen the grisly contents of that box because Peter Moore, to whom it had been delivered, had opened it in the privacy of his stateroom. But he had seen fit, somewhat later, to tell her what the box had contained.

It had been a hint, in grimly whimsical form, from the most powerful, most mysterious figure in China, to listen to nothing of what they had heard, to observe nothing of what they had seen, and above all, to repeat nothing of what they had heard and seen in his fabulous palace beneath the Lake of the Flying Dragon. In return for their secrecy, he had given them their lives.

Staring down at the little white jade symbol of the three great Chinese virtues, Susan O'Gilvie began to shiver. Across the street she heard, suddenly, the *clip-clop, clip-clop!* of those sandals. Since becoming aware that she was followed, Susan was quite certain that the man who wore the wooden sandals was a spy set upon her by that grotesque human creature who lived at the bottom of a lake. The Blue Scorpion!

But why was he having her followed? Did Mr. Lu wish to locate Peter Moore, whose adventures had given him fame as Peter the Brazen throughout China? Or was Mr. Lu merely having her watched, making sure that she lived up to her end of that strange tacit bargain?

As Susan stood before the jade shop, undecided whether to go in or go on, shivering from fear and cold, utterly wretched, the dim figure in the shop came nearer the window and looked out at her small white face. Susan, looking up, saw his glittering eyes. She was on the point of rushing in and asking him to send someone for a rickshaw. Then she saw his hand—a long, thin yellow hand with exceptionally long, pointed and incredibly dirty nails.

Like a disembodied hand, controlled by some mystic power, it floated down into the window. The fingers were bunched. The glimmer of light upon the hand made it appear to be scaled. It moved about with slow, graceful circlings, and Susan suddenly knew what it was that that hand reminded her of. A snake's head! It had the same slow, graceful motions, as if it were hovering, preparing to strike its prey.

Fascinated, Susan watched.

Slowly, with the utmost deliberation, the hand moved down until it was poised over the carving of the three jade monkeys. It had ignored the beautifully carved little idols, the amulets, the dozens of rare and ornamental chops, to select that carving of the three monkeys.

It seemed, like a striking snake, to pounce. Susan could see the glimmer of the man's eyes in the murk of the shop. Then she saw his teeth. They were yellow fangs. With the jade monkeys in his hand, he was grinning at her.

With a gasp, Susan stepped back from the window. A cold wet hand reaching out of the fog behind her could not have frightened her more. In a panic, she began to run. The fog had thickened. Bewildered and terror-stricken, Susan ran through the mud to a corner, turned and ran in the direction in which she was sure the river lay. If she could reach the river, she could find the bund. And once she reached the bund, she was safe.

Behind her, like an echo that would never cease, she heard the *clip-clop, clip-clop!* of the wooden sandals.

She turned another corner. A black dog came snarling out of the fog to snap at her heels. Susan kicked at him and ran on. Her throat was beginning to burn. There was a sharp, rising pain in her heart.

Far away she heard the whistle of a steamer, but she could not tell the direction from which it had come. The Whangpo wound like a great serpent about Shanghai, and sounds in the fog were deceiving.

She stopped and listened. The clacking of the sandals behind her was suddenly silenced. Listening, she heard nothing but the steady drip of water and, at a great distance, the faint clamor of cymbals.

She started toward the vague glow of a street lamp. Just under the lamp, she stepped on an object that was soft, that yielded. Looking down, she saw that she had stepped on a man, lying in the mud. A yellow man—a coolie. His throat was slashed. Blood was still oozing from this slash.

There was a pale blue mark on his forehead. A pale blue triangle! The mark of Mr. Lu! Susan stifled a scream and began to run again. She could turn in no direction, make no move, without coming face to face with some new evidence of Mr. Lu's imponderable power. Like this fog, coiling and winding about her, he was everywhere at once.

Suddenly—quite miraculously—Susan found the gate through which she had entered Chinese City a little more than a hour before. On Canton Road, a minute later, she called to a coolie jogging along between the shafts of an empty rickshaw. She climbed in and huddled down in a corner, shivering with cold, with apprehension—almost hysterical with terror.

She knew that the hand of the Blue Scorpion was reaching out for her. Was it about to strike? Was the Blue Scorpion toying with her before making the last fatal, horrible pounce? She had a strange, terrifying feeling that something frightful would happen that very night.

Susan wished that Peter Moore was in Shanghai. But she must keep on pretending that she had not the faintest idea of his whereabouts.

2

THE BLUE PYRAMID

IN A GUMWOOD shanty, two thousand miles from Shanghai, Peter Moore was at that moment looking for a blueprint. This particular blueprint showed, in elaborate detail, the arrangement of the buss-yard of the hydro-electric plant he was installing, high in the Shan Mountains, for the Ling Po Mining Company.

The Ling Po Mining Company was the project of a somewhat unusual individual, Dr. Hang Win, a man of some eighty years who had been, in the days of the Empire, a mandarin. He had weathered revolutions and wars, and was still one of the wealthiest men in China. He was determined, in his declining years, to put that wealth to good use.

Having visited the United States, and having marvelled at the amazing industrial developments which had taken place in that nation, he proposed to span, with one tremendous leap, a four-thousand-year handicap. For that section of China which lies at the headwaters of the mighty Yangtze Kiang is as backward as it was when, two thousand years before Christ, the first of its emperors ruled.

The owner of vast domains of valuable mining lands, Dr. Hang was, while not an easy customer, at least a likely prospect for tremendous quantities of electrical equipment. His schemes were, to say the least, ambitious. He wanted, to begin with, a hydro-electric plant for generating current which was to be transmitted over a high tension line for a distance of approximately four hundred miles to a copper mine. Then, over a distance of about three hundred miles in another direction, to an iron mine.

As the project represented an expenditure of millions of dollars, Peter Moore worked hard to secure the contract. There was, needless to say, the liveliest kind of competition. English, Belgian, German and other American firms were endeavoring to tempt Dr. Hang with a variety of bargains.

Peter Moore went about it, however, in another way. Having gone to some pains to learn all he possibly could about the rich mine owner, he spent two months in the saddle, studying the region over which Dr. Hang's power, like that of a feudal king, extended.

His proposition, when he finally presented it to the old mandarin, was to build, not the one hydro-electric plant, but two of them, and in addition, a steam-driven electric plant. His proposal was, further, to link these power stations into one great interlocking system, so that if one went out of commission for one reason or another—or even if two were out of commission—the doctor's enterprises would not suffer from a lack of electric power.

Moore's scheme was somewhat cleverer than it sounds when stated so flatly. He had discovered that the supply of water was greater in the eastern extremity of the doctor's territory than it was in the west; and he had also discovered that the facilities for impounding water in the western section were greater than in the east. The difficulty with the

western section was that the impounded water would be
at a level too low for satisfactory hydro-electric purposes.

His proposal, stated in another way, was to build a plant
in each section, with a third plant at the doctor's coal mine.
In the spring of the year the eastern plant would supply
current to the western one, so that the latter, with tremendous electrical pumps, could store water high in the hills
against the time when the water supply at the eastern plant
was low.

If there was a drouth in either section, the coal-burn-
ing plant would carry the load. And with the three plants
so situated, all of Dr. Hang's enterprises would be conveniently supplied with electric power at all times. With this
somewhat elaborate system, Moore confidently believed
shut-downs would be averted and there would be an excess
of power at all times.

It will be seen that his proposal would call for an expenditure perhaps more than three times greater than that
called for by any of the bids submitted by his competitors.
Dr. Hang accepted it because he saw in Peter Moore a man
of vision and imagination.

And so, backed by the almost unlimited financial and
manual resources of Dr. Hang, Moore had proceeded
with the eastern plant. Truly, the man-power placed at
his disposal was unlimited. Thousands and teeming thousands of up-country Chinese were placed at his bidding.
From the coast he imported some hundreds of Chinese
foremen and construction men who were familiar with
concrete work and steel building. He would have preferred
American foremen; but Dr. Hang, at this point, betrayed
his eccentricity.

Dr. Hang had bought the power plant equipment from the American electric company which Moore represented; and he had hired Moore to boss the building and the installation. That was because he believed that Americans are great engineers, and because he was "sold" on Moore.

But the real purpose of his tremendous investment was to give work to as many of the millions of China's unemployed as possible. He therefore wanted no white assistants; he insisted on Chinese. And accordingly Moore had hired Chinese to fill every post.

The American engineer had dealt with Chinese labor before, and he knew just what to expect from them. Trained Chinese, he had found, made excellent engineers, good bosses. And many of the young men on his staff had been trained in American or European universities. They knew electricity; they knew construction.

Work on Number One Plant, as the eastern unit was called, went forward smoothly and rapidly. A great dam was built. At the bottom of a five-hundred-foot gorge the plant was built.

But while all this industry was exciting great attention in that little-known part of China, Peter Moore had taken particular care that his own name be not identified with the project, and that his presence in that section of the country remain unknown to Mr. Lu. He was fully aware of the fact that Mr. Lu might at any moment make trouble for him. He lived, in fact, in hourly dread of such trouble. Yet he had taken every possible precaution to conceal his identity. And even if, despite his care, the reports should get back to Mr. Lu that Peter Moore was building a mysterious structure of steel and copper and reinforced concrete, Peter Moore was certain that Mr. Lu would not trouble him.

NUMBER ONE PLANT was, it was true, less than a thousand miles away from the Lake of the Flying Dragon and that fabulous subaqueous palace in which Mr. Lu lived. Yet the plant infringed in no wise on Mr. Lu's domain.

But he could not know whether or not Mr. Lu was in ignorance of his activity. The construction of the dam—in itself a gigantic piece of engineering in that part of the world—attracted thousands of curious sight-seers. Men on horseback. Men on camels. Whole tribes of wild plainsmen who came shouting and screaming.

They could understand the dam, but they could not understand the purpose of the complicated machinery which was being built into the plant at the foot of the dam. Why did that great steel pipe (the penstock) lead down into that white building? What was it going to do in there? What were these wires, strung on those massive pieces of porcelain, going to do?

It was impossible to explain electricity to these wild-minded men. To them it would become, and it would remain, white magic.

Dr. Hang lived in a hillside castle overlooking the shafts of his coal mine, two hundred miles from the Number One Plant. Steel poles, insulators and wires were already in place between the two. Transformers had been installed at the mine. Dr. Hang's house had been wired for lights and electric fans, against the parching heat of the desert winds. Moore wanted to open the wicket gates on a given date, so sending the water through the giant turbines—and electricity over those wires by the same date. With Moore, it was a matter of professional pride—and pocketbook.

He would, when that part of the job was finished, and if he made good on the day agreed upon, receive a cash bonus of five thousand dollars in gold; and he would also, he hoped, set at rest certain rumors that he wasn't good for much but adventuring. It was his ambition to become known as the foremost electrical engineer in China; and this was—if all went well—his chance.

Yet that was where the rub was. All was not going well. Little things were happening to delay him. The concrete mixture was wrong for a certain foundation. Certain essential parts which must travel upwards of nine thousand miles to reach him had vanished altogether—and must be replaced. Other shipments also mysteriously went astray.

All this had begun to happen within the last couple of weeks. Until then, everything had gone smoothly. He had hoped, in two more months, to have the job finished.

The latest of these annoyances was the vanishing of the buss-yard blueprint. A buss-yard is the steel-fenced enclosure adjoining a power plant, in which a layman sees merely a confusing forest of steel. In the buss-yard are the transformers, the lightning-arresters, certain of the circuit breakers, and other related machinery.

The layout for the Number One Plant buss-yard had been made in the engineering-department of the home office. And inasmuch as sixty thousand volts, stepped up from the thirteen thousand which the generators were to deliver to the buss-bars, would soon be hurtling out over the transmission wires, it was quite obviously necessary that the transformers, the arresters and the breakers be installed exactly in their proper relation.

One of Moore's young Chinese engineers could have duplicated the buss-yard blueprint in a week of work. But that was not the point. The point was that Peter Moore had placed that blueprint on a rack above his desk that very morning, and tonight it was gone.

Who had taken the blueprint? A check-up of the only men who could, with any stretch of the imagination, have been interested in that blueprint showed that none of them had touched it that day. No man had touched the buss-yard print; therefore it must be where Peter had left it. The only flaw in that logic was that the blueprint was not in that place.

Having searched his shack from end to end, even in the unlikeliest places, Moore gave it up and went outside for a solitary smoke before turning in.

It was the night of a green moon. Not yet emerged from its first quarter, this moon poured down a mild emerald radiance into the cañon, glittering on quartz and mica shale, giving the whole scene a ghostly look. A cold night wind fell from the dam into the river bottom, as water falls.

Thinking of the missing blueprint, Peter's thoughts joined those of Susan, two thousand miles away, in the contemplation of a grisly memory—the embalmed heads of three red-haired men packed neatly into a sapphire-blue box. "Hear no evil—see no evil—speak no evil!"

Certainly, he had fulfilled his part of that fantastic agreement with the fabulous monster who lived in a castle at the bottom of a lake. He had said nothing of that strange adventure to any one. Yet, in spite of his elaborate precautions, he was now almost certain that since that night not a moment had passed when he had not been under observation.

He knew that the Blue Scorpion, out of his grimly, whimsical nature, had spared his and Susan O'Gilvie's lives, just as he knew that if either of them breathed a word of what they had seen, of what had happened in that incredible underwater palace, death would come instantly—and in some dreadful form—to both!

Puffing at his pipe, Peter Moore wondered what Susan was doing at this moment. She had spoken of going to Manila, to visit friends. She might, she had said, decide to go to Japan for the cherry blossom festivals. She wouldn't, she believed, stay in China. It would be safer, they had agreed, if she left China for a time. He had no means of knowing what she was doing. She knew where he was, but they had agreed it would be wise if she did not write to him, or he to her. She was quite as anxious for him to make good on the hydro-electric project as he was himself.

It had been many months—it actually seemed years— since he had seen that beautiful and exciting young woman. He missed her. He missed her much more than he cared to admit. He missed her gaiety, her jauntiness, her enthusiasm. Perhaps, most of all, he missed those moments when she was demure and sweet—and not looking for excitement.

Puffing at his pipe, he could see her face quite clearly— her large eyes, which were not blue, but a deep, true violet; the alluring line of her chin; her lovely red lips. Susan was beautiful. Seeing her so clearly, he suddenly could hear her voice, sweet and clear and thrilling; could see and hear her, caught in the yearning of an eager mood, softly laughing, saying: "I think it's perfectly fascinating!"

He sighed comfortably. He wished Susan was there. She'd love that place. But he was glad she wasn't in China. He was glad she was safe—in Manila or Japan. And he wished that he was in Japan with her, "doing" the cherry-blossom festivals, drinking thick grass-green tea with her, eating little white sugar cakes.

Something fell softly in the shale at his feet. He glanced down, and the light of the green quarter moon helped him to find the object.

He picked it up in his fingers. It was a perfect pyramid of pale blue chalk, not more than three-eighths of an inch high—the sign of the Blue Scorpion!

The American glanced up at the sheer wall of the cañon. He saw no one. Something like an icy little wind tingled along his backbone. The beauty had suddenly departed from the night. The cañon became black and sinister all at once.

Again, but dubiously this time, Peter Moore wondered what Susan O'Gilvie was doing.

3

LEAVING AT DAWN

SUSAN O'GILVIE WAS, at that moment, standing under a cold shower in the bathroom of her suite in the Astor House Hotel. She was trying to shock her nerves into a state of steadiness.

Returning to the hotel from that dismaying experience in Chinese City, she had realized that she had only a little time to bathe and dress for the dinner party that Dr. Luigi Strang and his wife were giving for her and Bill Montgomery. Since her unpleasantness with Bill Montgomery at the French Consulate cocktail party, she wished that she might avoid that dinner party for four. She was sorry for Bill, but she was just as sorry for herself. And in her present state of nerves—bordering hysteria—she could not contemplate the dinner party with the slightest of pleasure.

But it was too late now to decline the invitation, and she was rather anxious to see Dr. Strang and his wife again, and at close quarters. They were Americans, and she felt the need of being with her countrymen this evening. At the same time, they revolted her. Therefore, being the capricious person that she was, Susan found the Strangs fascinating.

But she must get herself in hand before she met them,

and the quickest way, she had found, of calming a set of jittering nerves was to stand under an icy shower until she was practically numb.

The shower did steady her, but as she rubbed herself with a large rough towel, she knew that the steadying effect was only temporary. She could still hear, in her lively imagination, the *clip-clop, clip-clop!* of those relentless sandals; she could see the snake-like hand of the man in the jade shop as he picked up the carving of the three monkeys; she could feel the yielding softness of that dead coolie upon whom she had trod under the street light; and she could smell the dismal, sour smells of Chinese City in the billowing tawny fog.

Susan decided to wear her sapphire blue dinner gown, with its matching satin slippers. The heels of the slippers were crusted with Chantaboun sapphires. Jeweled heels were a weakness, a vanity, of Susan's. She had beautifully small feet. She shod them in the costliest shoes available, and she loved sparkling heels. Once, in Hong Kong, a diamond-crusted heel of hers had almost cost her her life. China was not a safe place in which to wear jeweled heels, but caution was not among Susan's virtues.

She selected the sapphire gown and slippers for the Strangs' dinner party, with unconscious, or perhaps deliberate, cruelty. It clasped her slim and beautiful figure in a fashion that made her enchanting, alluring, bewitching. That gown would reduce Bill Montgomery almost to a state of suicidal despair! She could have worn a gown that was less revealing, less seductive. But she would not have been a woman if she had.

When Susan had arranged her beautiful dark hair to

her liking, and was satisfied with the subtle allure of her make-up, she struggled into the blue silk garment. The excitement she had undergone in Chinese City, followed by that shocking cold shower, had given her eyes a gem-like brilliance. She turned slowly, on her sapphire-crusted heels, before a long mirror, and she had to admit that she had never looked so marvelous. Her suppressed air of excitement, due to the hysterical condition of her nerves; her fine coloring, due only slightly to cosmetics, would have made her, tonight, the belle of any ball.—Yet she hoped it would be a very calm, uneventful evening.

A sudden, insistent hammering at the door of her parlor, which adjoined her bedroom, distracted her from the appreciation of her slim elegance. But it did more than that. It gave her nerves a bad moment, a sickening twitch, so proving that they were not nearly so well in hand as she had hoped.

Susan had bolted and locked that door when she came in. Now she unbolted it. But before she turned the key, she called, "Who is it?"

A gruff masculine voice answered, "It's me."

"Bill?"

"Yes—Bill." Uncompromisingly hurt.

"Oh, Lord!" Susan said, but not loud enough for him to hear.

She unlocked the door. Bill Montgomery towered at the threshold—six feet and several inches of handsome and indignant American manhood. He had evidently just come in from the street. His thick, curly black hair was wet and wild. His shoes and his trousers were black and gray with wet and drying mud. There were specks of mud on his flushed cheeks. There was a smear of mud along his chin.

Towering over her, he declared in a thick, angry voice, "What a hell of a trick to play on a man!"

"Did you get lost?" she said meekly.

"Of course I got lost!"

"Well, so did I, Bill."

He was, she perceived, really furious. He declared she had made him ridiculous before all those people.

"You shouldn't have tried to hold my hand before them, then."

"Can I help it," he cried savagely, "because I'm mad about you?"

One black curl was plastered down on his forehead. He was one of the handsomest men, in a strictly romantic way, she had ever seen. He should have gone into the movies, or on the stage. He was, by far, the most emotional man she had ever known.

Bill Montgomery reminded Susan of an actor, a juvenile in a romantic comedy, or a musical comedy. His voice was deep and resonant. He was always dashing about, making gestures; thumping his heart, declaiming. Dramatic passion welled up in him from a seemingly inexhaustible spring. His face was always darkly flushed. His lips were crisp and very red. His deep blue eyes, when he became aroused, turned hotly black.

He was ardent, more than slightly spoiled; given to sullen brooding and bursts of magnificent, really poetic temper. He had been a football hero. Susan had seen women gaze at him dreamily, with that speculative look, and sigh deeply, tremulously. He was almost any woman's ideal, romantic lover.

At this moment Susan was more than a little afraid of him. He was such a powerful, such a headstrong young man. And he looked so wrathful. He had come in and slammed the door. Now he strode down the room and came striding back. He placed his great, broad-shouldered bulk in front of Susan. His fists were clenched at his sides. Her head, if she had been inclined to verify her guess, would have come to the top of his collar.

Bill Montgomery's father was a cattle king in Montana. Bill was taking a round-the-world trip, preparatory to settling down as a cattle prince.

He had met Susan at a dance at the British Embassy, in Peiping; had followed her to Shanghai. He hadn't given her any peace since.

"What difference does it make if I make love to you before all the people in the world?"

"Only that I hate being demonstrative in public."

"But I love you so—My God, Susan, you don't seem to realize that. I should be on my way. I've got to be home in two months.—You've got to say you'll come with me!"

SUSAN WAS AFRAID he was going to sweep her into his arms. He had done that once before.

"You don't realize how you're making me suffer, Susan. You're all I can think about. You've got to tell me you love me!"

"Bill, we're due at the Strangs' in fifteen minutes. You haven't any more time to waste."

"Damn the Strangs! I'd a thousand times rather spend the evening alone with you.—Oh, Susan, you're so damned beautiful! Why did I have to meet you? You've ruined my life."

Susan told him, rather sharply, to stop being so silly.

" 'Silly'!" he roared. "My God! Don't you see I'm eating my heart out?" He thumped his heart with a large brown fist. "Don't you realize that I'll die if I don't have you?"

His lips were parted slightly. He was breathing through them.

"That's the gown you wore the night I met you. I can see you now, coming down those stairs. I'd just been dancing with that terrible Bruzzia girl—and there you were. I'd never, in my life, seen anything so lovely—so slim. You might have walked out of a dream.—Darling! Let's duck this damned dinner. Let's go somewhere and dance!"

Susan firmly shook her head.

Bill Montgomery clamped his lips together. He turned and strode down the room. Approaching her again, he lifted one clenched fist as if he were about to strike her.

He stopped a few feet away and said, with a deep groan, "Susan, this is the end!—I'm leaving tomorrow for India."

Susan knew that it was impossible for him not to be dramatic. He must use such phrases as "This is the end," "I'm leaving—for India." He pronounced it "In-jah."

"Isn't this a bit sudden?" Susan meekly asked.

"There's a P. & O. boat clearing at dawn," he answered. "I realize how futile it's been. I've made an ass of myself. But I thought you'd relent."

"I'm sorry," Susan said, and sincerely meant it.

"I understand," he whispered.

It must hurt him, Susan reflected, terribly. She'd seen those other women, wherever they went, staring at him.

Such a good looking young man—with his romantic fervor—could have had almost any woman he chose. By a snap of the finger! She was probably the first girl he had ever known who had not positively adored him.—She liked him, yes. She thought he was tremendously attractive. He appealed, however, not to Susan's heart but to her sense of humor.

"If it wasn't so early," Susan said, "I'd get up and see you off.—But dawn!" She shivered.

Why, Susan wondered, didn't she sensibly fall in love with an attractive young man like Bill Montgomery? Why was she, herself, so hopelessly, romantically, in love with that gray-eyed young engineer two thousand miles away in the Shan Hills?

She hoped Bill Montgomery would not try to kiss her good-by. That would only make things worse.

He went to the door. He was no longer wrathful. He was terribly hurt.

"I suppose," he said, "it means—good-by forever!"

4

WAS IT ALL PLANNED?

KAREN STRANG WAS, Susan believed, one of the women whom Bill Montgomery could have had by snapping his fingers. This was strange, in a way, because Karen Strang was a bride of not much more than five or six months.

She was the most fascinating woman Susan had ever met. She was blond, blue-eyed and slim; a little taller than Susan. And her eyes were the worldliest eyes that Susan had ever seen. Large and pale blue, they were as brilliant—and quite as opaque—as porcelain. They went, somehow, with the rest of her. It was as if Mrs. Strang wore, over her true self, a thin, very hard shell. That was the effect she gave, at least to Susan—one of brilliance and hardness.

Karen Strang's hair was of that rare blond shade which is truly golden. Every lock of it was always in place. It was more like a cap of metallic gold than human hair. And in its smooth, flawless arrangement it was quite characteristic of the woman, as Susan had come to know her during the past week. Mrs. Strang was suave and finished. She was never ill at ease. Her charm was of the cool kind—the charm of perfect, imperious poise.

Because of these facts, Susan found Karen Strang fascinating. She realized that she might know the woman for ten or twenty years, yet never really know her. Karen's feelings, her personal reactions, her emotions were lived behind that thin, hard glaze with which she coated herself.

Susan would not have trusted Mrs. Strang any farther than she could have thrown her by that cap of flawless golden hair. Susan considered her an extremely dangerous woman. Her coldness, her hardness, made her fascinating—as a reptile is fascinating.

But her husband was of another type entirely. Dr. Luigi Strang looked so downright villainous that Susan found him enchanting. He reminded her of a Kodiak bear. He had shaggy brown hair and a shaggy brown beard. His black eyes were red-rimmed, and his bright red lips, seen through the beard, were always moist. He was always wetting them. His eyes, lacking pupils, because of their inky blackness, gave him a hypnotic look.

The Strangs were an unusual pair, but Susan had found that the Far East abounded in unusual pairs, and she had long ago given up trying to reason out why this man had married that woman, or vice versa. She always thought of the Strangs as she would have thought of a snake and a bear—an unusual combination to be found anywhere. She wondered why a wom-an as fastidious as Karen Strang had married such a shaggy looking man. And she wondered what the doctor thought of his bride's quite obvious interest in Bill Montgomery.

The Strangs were taking a leisurely honeymoon about the Far East, where Karen's parents had spent the last year of their lives. She had met Dr. Strang in Mexico, and they had been married in Mexico City. Dr. Strang's residence was San Bernardino, California, where he owned and conducted a sanitarium for what he described, carelessly, as "brain cases." He was always very vague about it. He called himself a psycho-pathologist, and Susan sometimes wondered if he didn't lean a little toward the art of hypnotism. He looked as if he could be brutal without half trying. Sometimes when he stared at her he reminded her of *Svengali*. In any case, she was quite sure that Karen Strang was not playing *Trilby*.

It also seemed to Susan that Dr. Luigi Strang fixed his eyes upon her a little too frequently, and for rather overlong periods. She would catch him staring at her ankles, at her neck, with a look of greediness that was not at all becoming to a bridegroom of only a few months. He made Susan a little uneasy. Actually, he revolted her. She thought he was, behind those staring, red-rimmed eyes and that uncouth bushiness, behind those too-ardent red lips, a kind of monster. Wherefore, being Susan, she was fascinated.

But at least the Strangs were compatriots, and she relished the chance of being close to her own countrymen tonight. The effects of her icy shower both were wearing off. Perhaps Bill Montgomery, with his intensity, had helped to wear them off. At all events, when Susan left her room and started for the Strangs' suite, she was conscious of being very nervous, very jumpy.

The Strangs' suite was on the floor above hers. The doctor had suggested having dinner served there because the hotel dining room was so cold and cheerless.

A CHINESE BOY, the Strangs' personal servant, let Susan in. Dr. Strang, in long tails, was engaged in shaking cocktails in a hammered silver affair.

His big, sloping shoulders were jogging up and down.

He had very white hands—as white as a woman's—and the backs were covered with black hair. They were the slim, delicate hands of a surgeon, incongruous in relation to his barrel-like body, and had it not been for their hairiness would have attracted Susan.

As he stood there, jogging away with the cocktail shaker, Susan tried to picture him in a bathing suit. The vision was so grotesque that Susan giggled.

His black eyes stared at her loveliness. They ran slowly down from her slim white shoulders to the blue satin slippers with their sapphire heels.

"You are very lovely indeed, Susan!" he said, in his deep, thick, somewhat guttural voice.

Susan wondered if his beard had any effect on his voice.

He walked toward her, shaking the silver shaker more slowly. "My wife is still dressing," he said in a lower voice, as if he were pressing confidences upon her. He paused for a moment. "I have never seen you so beautiful. I have never seen any one in my life even half so beautiful! You have that rare quality, my dear—a brightly flaming spirit. Your philosophy is in your eyes—*toujours de l'audace!*"

Always audacious! "Not always!" Susan demurely corrected him.

But Dr. Strang was evidently determined to make the most of this enchanted moment.

To her it was as if some one had set loose discordant, jarring vibrations. She was accustomed to having men make love to her; she fended men off in the usual ways. Compared to this man, Bill Montgomery would be as easy as a child to handle.

Their shoulders were almost touching now. Susan was

standing with her back against a table. She could not move farther back without tipping the table over. Dr. Strang's eyes came closer to hers, until they were like large pools of India ink.

Susan suddenly began to tremble. Her jumpy nerves could not stand much of this sort of thing. Yet she could not move away without touching him, and the thought of touching him was loathsome.

"My dear—" he whisperingly began.

Susan hardly heard the words. Dropping her eyes, she saw his red, wet lips move and form the words.

Karen's brilliant, silken voice cut in upon what he was about to say. "Is that you, Susan? What are you two quarreling about?"

As Dr. Luigi Strang stepped back, it struck Susan that his wife was being a little too tactful.

"Susan was criticizing my cocktails," the doctor said easily—much too easily.

And Susan sensed, as she had on previous moments, that the strange doctor and his strange wife were hardly keeping up a pretense of being in love. And Susan was still young enough to wonder why people married if it wasn't for love.

Karen told Susan she looked simply too delicious. "I don't wonder that every man in Shanghai is mad about you, darling."

Sweet and smooth and silken! Susan, murmuring, was struck afresh by Karen Strang's cold, slim beauty. It actually seemed to glitter. In the coolest possible shade of green, which is jade, Karen, Susan remarked to herself, *was* a jade—and jaded lady. There were jade ornaments on her green slippers, and she wore about her snow-white throat a string of kingfisher jade. The individual pieces were amulets. Chinese for love!

Dr. Strang asked where Bill Montgomery was.

"I think he's dressing," Susan said, carelessly.

"Didn't you go to a cocktail party with him?" Karen asked.

Susan, looking at the woman's marvelous golden hair, nodded.

"Are you going to marry that young man?" the doctor wanted to know.

Susan's definite, firm "No," was lost in a sharp clatter of knuckles on the door. The noise made her start. She wished that she could pull herself together. She wished that Dr. Strang would not look at her shoulders with those greedy black eyes.

It was Bill Montgomery, dark and handsome and romantic in dinner clothes. Susan wondered why it was that if men were romantic at all they looked so much more so in dinner jackets.

Bill was enacting a different part now. His air was sad and preoccupied. Doubtless, since she had sent him away, he had been brooding himself into that rôle. His eyes, when they at length found Susan's, verified this. They were the dark, fathomless eyes of tragedy. They seemed to say, "You—you have done this to me!"

And Susan was tempted to say, aloud, "Ah, *Romeo*— poor *Romeo!*"

The cocktails were dry Martinis, which, the doctor declared, marked the apex reached by this Babylonian civilization. He, himself, he said, preferred Sandeman's Oporto Blanco—but people no longer drank wines for apéritifs.

There was a queer, Oriental after-flavor in the cocktail that made Susan uneasy. But perhaps it was her nerves. She was certain she detected an electrical tension in the air, but this she also credited to her imagination.

KAREN STRANG WANTED to know if the party at the French Consulate had been interesting.

"Very much so," Bill Montgomery said grimly, "for every one concerned.—Susan ran away."

"Bill!" Susan said.

"I'm sorry, my dear," the young man persisted, fixing his dark, melancholy eyes on her eyes, "but you did run away. You objected to my holding your hand in public. So," he went on, addressing Karen now, "Susan bolted—ducked—beat it—blew!"

"The word," Susan said, with an effort at lightness, "is 'scrammed.'—I scrammed.—Then we both got lost in Chinese City. Lots of people were killed. Sirens blew. Fireworks went off. It was all very confusing."

But Dr. Strang wasn't smiling. His black eyes seemed to bore through hers and to smoke out the secrets behind them.

He finally shook his head, with a baffled air. "I don't understand you, Susan. To my way of thinking, Bill is the most eligible young man on either side of the Pacific. And you treat him like a door mat."

"That," Bill said gloomily, "is because I place myself in the doormat position."

"I think," the doctor said, "that you belong in the psychopathic ward, Susan. What do you think, Karen?"

"I've always thought," the jade lady answered, "that every

girl has the right to select the man she loves.—But how can any girl resist Bill? I know I can't."

"The trouble with Susan," Bill said, "is that she's in love with somebody else. I haven't a chance."

Susan was clenching her fists behind her, telling herself to stay cool and calm and collected. But if this kept up much longer she would start smashing things.

She tried to change the subject. Had Karen been shopping today?

The jade lady was evasive, indifferent.

The attitudes of these three people almost made Susan suspect that this was a conspiracy—a conspiracy to force her into the arms of the handsome, wretched Bill. She wondered if he had, as an unrequited lover's last resort, presented his woes to the Strangs, and implored their cooperation.

Whatever was behind all this, it was, Susan thought, in rotten bad taste. She couldn't stand much more of it.

But they wouldn't let her change the subject. Dr. Strang, pouring "dividends," mentioned that Bill was handsome, rich, and came from a distinguished family.

"What do you suppose money counts with Susan?" Bill groaned. "Isn't she the richest girl in America? She could buy out Henry Ford!"

"I bought him out yesterday," Susan said promptly. "I'm going to revolutionize his car." She wanted to say she was going to change the Ford into a juggernaut for trampling down people who tried to force girls into marrying men they didn't care about. But she had to give her host and hostess the benefit of the doubt. Perhaps her nerves were transforming pleasantries into infuriating insults. She must try to control herself.

"No, the real trouble with Susan," Dr. Strang said, "is that she's in love with some worthless, fortune-hunting adventurer."

5

HALLUCINATIONS.

SUSAN WANTED TO shriek at the doctor. If this kept up much longer.

"A fellow named Peter Moore," Bill said. "I've heard about him."

"Who hasn't?" the doctor demanded. "You can't be in China twenty-four hours without hearing about him. It's men like him that give the United States such a ridiculous reputation abroad.—But I can't believe that a girl as intelligent as Susan is seriously interested in a man like him."

"Let's drop it," Bill said. "Susan is getting riled."

But Dr. Strang had no intention of dropping it.

"Susan, why don't you stop wasting your fragrance on that desert rat and marry good old Bill?"

"As far as I'm concerned," Susan said tensely, "there is only one man in the world. Will you please stop picking on him?"

"But he's a fortune hunter!" the doctor said. "All he wants is your money."

"Really?" Susan said faintly. She had been quarreling with Peter Moore for almost two years because he wouldn't have her, in spite of her wealth. That fortune, in fact, was his only objection to her. Her wealth was a mountainous barrier between them.

Dr. Strang, perhaps sensing that she stood on firm ground here, shifted his attack. They were at dinner now. Peter Moore lived, the doctor declared, only to make people talk about his preposterous adventures.

Susan, sitting there white-faced, bright-lipped, angry-eyed, tried to be calm. She couldn't eat a thing. Bill Montgomery, at first puzzled by the doctor's tactics, at last became angry; he tried to spare Susan.

But the doctor evidently had a one-track mind. Didn't Susan realize that Moore was an absolutely irresponsible character? Didn't she realize that he was a drifter—in a class with beach combers? That he was actually nothing but a cheap bum? Didn't she realize what life would be like with a worthless creature like him?

"And none too scrupulous, either," the doctor heavily added. "Now, Karen, what was it you heard yesterday?"

"Don't you think," Karen answered sweetly, "that you've ridden Susan long enough?"

Susan was grateful, but she wondered if Karen really meant that. She wished Peter was there. He would silence this shaggy brute in a dozen sizzling words.

"I'll refresh your memory," Dr. Strang said, obtusely. "That chap from the embassy told you that all these things we hear about Moore are preposterous lies—products of his wild imagination.—Adventures? Bah! That man would kill a defenseless coolie and make an Arabian Nights fable out of it! He is probably the greatest liar in China—and heaven knows he has lively competition!"

"That isn't so!" Susan cried. Her eyes blazed. "I've known

him for almost two years. I've seen things—" She stopped. She mustn't talk, yet her nerves were driving her to talk. In another moment she would be hysterical. "Don't you suppose, doctor, I'm old enough to know my own mind?"

"I've known intelligent people of sixty," he answered, "who never knew their own minds. Few of us know our own minds.—No, my dear. You are a lonely girl. This is a dangerous country. You're a thrill hunter. This fellow Moore is very cleverly supplying you with a cheap imitation of the real thing."

Susan's hands were clutched in her lap. She was trying not to tremble. Her eyes felt hot. She wondered if she was on the verge of a nervous breakdown. She wished, again, that Peter Moore was there. He wouldn't let this shaggy brute torment her so.

Bill Montgomery was doing his best, interrupting, arguing. But he seemed puzzled, even dazed.

"I'VE NEVER HEARD such amazing lies," the doctor was saying, staring blackly at Susan. "Products of a diseased imagination! The latest is that he came to grips with some fantastic Chinese monster, in human form, I think, who rules China with an invisible hand. The name of this monster, they say, is Mr. Lu. If Moore came to my sanitarium for observation, I'd lock him in a padded cell. The man's positively dangerous!"

Susan said hysterically, uncontrollably, "But there is such a person!"

"What, Susan? What?"

"I tell you, there is!—I've seen him!"

"Oh! Oh! You haven't seen Mr. Lu!"

"I have!—We both saw him!"

"Oh, no, Susan! It was hypnosis."

"It was real!" she panted. "I saw him. We both saw him!"

"Not really, my dear!" He was mocking her now, egging her on. "Tell me! Is it true that this amazing Mr. Lu lives in a palace at the bottom of a lake?—Don't tell me that's true, my dear!"

"It is true!" the distracted girl cried. "Peter Moore rescued me from that horrible place!"

"Don't tell me you were all through that fabulous place!"

"I was. He captured me!"

"Ah, yes! This man, Mr. Lu—don't they call him the Blue Scorpion?"

"They do! That's the truth! We were tricked to that lake by a man named Wong. Wong was after the Blue Scorpion's treasure. I was captured and taken down there. Peter Moore rescued me!"

She was so weak, so hysterical, she could hardly form the words. But the eyes of Dr. Strang remained incredulous, mocking.

"Tell us about the underwater palace!"

"I was blindfolded.—You see this scar on my arm? That's where I got it."

It was as if she was saying all this against her will. She couldn't check herself. She was aware that Bill Montgomery was staring at her; that his face was suddenly gray. Not until long afterward did she recall how Karen Strang kept sending meaning glances at her husband, how she kept toying with the chain of jade about her throat.

A sense of alarm suddenly filled Susan. She had broken her promise. In spite of herself, in spite of her resolutions, she had broken her promise. She had violated the warning implicit in the embalmed heads of the three red-headed men. "Hear no evil—see no evil—*speak* no evil."

Susan sprang up, grasping the edge of the table, swaying, fiercely biting her lip. She clasped her hands to her spinning head.

"Listen!" she said faintly. "I shouldn't have said that. I promised I'd say nothing to any one about it.—I can trust you, can't I? Will you promise me you won't repeat a word of what I've said to a living soul?—Doctor! It's terribly important."

"Why, of course, my dear!"

"Karen?"

"Susan, you poor darling, I wouldn't dream—"

"Bill?"

They had all risen. Bill was staring at her incredulously. For perhaps the first time since she had known him, he was not dramatizing himself. He was simply a shocked young man. His voice was strange and thick. "You know I won't repeat it, Susan."

"Karen, I'll have to be excused," Susan said. "I—I'm just all in. Good night and—and thank you so much!"

"I'll take you to your room," Bill said.

He took her arm. At the door, he turned and sent an angry but perplexed glance at the Strangs. Perhaps he wanted to tell Dr. Strang what he thought of him.

But he said nothing except, "I won't be back." He was in very deep water.

Susan said good night to him at the door. She wouldn't let him come in, and she wouldn't answer his questions.

She unlocked her door and dazedly switched on the lights. Everything was blurred and queer. Everything was a thin blue mist. She tottered into her bedroom and threw herself, face down, on the bed.

Susan let herself go. She sobbed. She shivered. The one thing she wanted in the world was to see Peter, to be close to him. With him, she was never afraid.

Simultaneously, she grew conscious of two things. One spot on the linen of the pillow into which she was sobbing was stiffer and harder than the rest of it. Her other discovery was that she was the victim of a hallucination. It was the light in the room. The light wasn't white, but rather a ghastly, dreadful blue—the blue of corpses!

Susan, pushing herself up on her elbows, uttered a faint cry of terror. The light was blue! Some one had changed all the bulbs from white to blue—this ghastly blue!

She glanced down at the sheet of paper on her pillow, slightly crumpled by her arm, slightly wet with her tears. On it was written in tall, thin letters, in pale blue chalk, he one word, *"Death!"*

With a little scream, she started up from the bed. Then she shrank back. In the middle of the room stood a man! A tall, lean man. A Chinese, in pale blue robes. His arms were folded on his chest. In the eerie blue light his face, with its narrow, pointed chin, was a blue triangle—chalked or painted a ghastly pale blue.

Susan's teeth were chattering. In a shuddering gasp, "Who—are you?" she demanded.

The apparition did not answer.

"How did you get in here?—What do you want?"

Not a muscle moved in that terrifying blue face.

"Say something!" Susan screamed.

The blue lips parted. The apparition uttered a single word, in a low, rasping voice:—

"*Death!*"

6

HURRIED DEPARTURE

DR. LUIGI STRANG was pacing up and down the room, smoking a short, thick black cigar. Occasionally he glanced at his watch. Occasionally he glanced at his wife. She lay back in a chaise longue, one hand holding a scented cigarette in a long white jade holder, the fingers of the other toying with the string of carved jade about her neck.

Every time he passed the table, the doctor would shake ashes into one of the plates of food. He said nothing. He seemed deeply engrossed in thought.

Karen Strang was gazing dreamily at the table at which she and her husband and Susan O'Gilvie and Bill Montgomery had recently been sitting. Her plucked golden brows were delicate arches, like the wings of a pouncing bird. Not once did she glance at this shaggy-haired, shaggy-bearded man who was her husband.

They were waiting.

The corridor door presently opened and a tall, thin Chinese in blue robes slipped in. His face was streaked faintly with blue, as if he had recently wiped off a coating of blue chalk, or blue grease, or paint, and had left these traces.

"That missy," he stated in a low, rasping voice, "she packee. B'long time go away. Savvy?"

Dr. Strang clapped his hands together. He was grinning delightedly. "It worked!" he exclaimed. "Karen, there's no doubt about it. She's going to him. It's the only place in the world she would be going. Get packed!"

"But she can't be leaving tonight!" the jade lady protested.

"Certainly she's leaving tonight! She's leaving as fast as she can!"

"But there aren't any more trains!"

"There are half a dozen river steamers, aren't there?"

"Can they leave in this fog?"

"Fog," the Chinese said, "allatime gone."

"How long will we be gone?" Karen asked.

"God only knows. Perhaps weeks!"

"But you aren't going without Avery Van Zant!"

"No, my dear. Avery will be here any moment. His train got in a half hour ago. He will come immediately here."

Karen Strang arose. "Very well. But I expected a cable-gram from mother tomorrow. I'll go down and cable her that we'll be out of touch for some time. I'll be right back."

"Don't be long."

"No, dear."

Mrs. Strang slipped out of the room. Once in the hall, she began to run. Picking up her jade-green dress, so that she would not trip, she ran as if she were pursued by demons. She did not pause at the lift, but proceeded on to the stairs. On clicking heels she ran down the stairs.

Reaching the lobby, she did not go to the desk where cablegram and radiograph blanks were. She did not even glance in that direction. Instead, regardless of the stares that centered upon her, she proceeded through the crowded lobby to the door which gave upon Whangpoo

Road. Ignoring the tall, red-turbaned Sikh doorman, she walked rapidly out upon Whangpoo Road and proceeded to the Garden Bridge.

The fog, as the Chinese had told her husband, was clearing. But wisps of it, like disembodied spirits, still rose in spots from the churning brown river, and drifted eerily past street lights. At the intersection of Soochow and the bund, she waited. She waited, with the chill wind from the river blowing upon her bare shoulders, for perhaps forty seconds. Then, from the purple darkness of Soochow Road, a sound came—the *clip-clop, clip-clop!* of wooden sandals. A spidery man, a bent and twisted coolie with one shoe-button eye, came toward her. His other eye was gone. In place of it was an inflamed socket.

She whispered two short sentences to him in Chinese. The shoe-button eye stared at her a moment, then the spidery man nodded, turned about and walked away. *Clip-clop, clip-clop.*

Mrs. Strang returned quickly to the hotel. She went to the lift. As it climbed, she coolly contemplated herself in one of the mirrors. Her porcelain blue eyes betrayed no excitement. Her color was unchanged. Not a thread of her remarkable golden hair was disarranged.

The suite, when she reentered it, was a scene of confusion. Her husband was packing. He was throwing things into bags and suitcases. But he stopped when Karen came in and regarded her with angry black eyes.

"Why were you gone so long?"

"I'm so dumb," she said sweetly, "about cablegrams. I always try to write exactly ten words. I'm sorry."

She helped him with his things and began packing her own.

"We'll store the trunks here," he said. "We're going to travel light."

"Where is Professor Van Zant?"

The doctor said irritably, "I don't know. Maybe you will have to go on without me."

Karen Strang laid out the clothes she would wear. "Luigi, don't you think this is rather a crazy scheme? We will have to travel on the same boat with that girl. She will see us. She's bound to see us. She will know we are following her. She won't go to him."

The doctor told her irritably to leave those details to him.

They finished packing. And when Mrs. Strang had changed to a blue suit, they went down to the lobby, their Chinese boy carrying their luggage.

At the desk Dr. Strang learned that Miss O'Gilvie had already left. She had evidently thrown a few things into a bag and fled. The clerk did not know where she had gone. She had not bought a steamship ticket, so far as he knew.

The doctor blamed his wife. If she had not taken so long over that damned cablegram, they would not have missed Susan. But the Sikh doorman gave them hope. He said that Miss O'Gilvie had taken a rickshaw to the landing stages on Northern Yangtze Road.

"But which one?"

The clerk did not know. Dr. Strang and his wife took rickshaws and directed their coolies to the landing stages along Northern Yangtze Road. The doctor was furious. His plans had missed fire. It was absolutely necessary for him to see Professor Van Zant; and it was absolutely necessary for him to know where Susan O'Gilvie was going. Without that information, his whole scheme was spoiled.

He snarled at the rickshaw coolies to hurry. He puffed furiously at his black stub of cigar. His strange eyes, under the street lights, were not black but crimson. They seemed to smolder and to flash.

At the junction of Tsingpoo Road and Northern Yangtze, there was an unexpected diversion. The doctor and his wife simultaneously espied a man lying in the mud under a street lamp. Even in that poor light, it could be seen that the recumbent figure was not a native, but a white man. A white man in dinner dress!

Karen cried, "It's Billy!"

She shrieked at her rickshaw boy to stop.

7

THE CRYSTAL GAZER

BOTH RICKSHAWS STOPPED. While Dr. Strang climbed heavily out of his, Karen scrambled down. When the doctor reached her, she was kneeling in the mud, regardless of the fact that it would soil her dress. She had Bill Montgomery's head in her hands, was frantically tugging at him, shaking him, hysterically repeating his name.

If Susan could have seen her then, she would have realized that there were moments when the jade lady could lose her poise, when the glaze of her self-possession seemed to be fractured.

Her husband took her hysteria as a matter of course, as if he was aware that she was infatuated with this handsome romantic. He did not appear to care in the least.

Bill Montgomery's face was as white as death. His eyes were closed. There was an ugly, rather deep cut on the left side of his forehead from which blood darkly pulsed. The doctor examined his eyes, pushed his hysterical wife away, and placed his ear to the young man's chest.

He lifted his head and said, "He's been knocked out. He must have been with Susan."

The doctor placed his thumbs at the base of the young man's brain, encircled his throat with his thin, surgeon's fingers, as if he planned to strangle him. His wife watched him with frightened blue eyes. But Dr. Strang did not strangle the young man. He felt about the base of his skull with his thumbs for a moment, then sharply pressed.

As if, with a knowledge of dark magic, he had pressed upon the very nerve of life, he caused Bill Montgomery's eyes to pop open. The young man groaned, took one deep breath, then another. He stared at Karen, then at Dr. Strang. He tried to get to his feet. The doctor helped him up.

Bill Montgomery dashed the blood from his left eye with the back of his hand, and gasped, "They got her!" He swayed.

Dr. Strang said sharply, "Get hold of yourself! What happened?"

"Susan telephoned my room. She said she was leaving—wanted me to take her down to the landing stages."

"Which one?—Which one?"

"She didn't say."

"Didn't she say where she was going?"

"No. We started down. We got this far. A gang of men in blue mask's came swarming out of that road. They grabbed her. I tried to fight. One of them hit me in the head with something."

"Where did they take her?"

"I don't know." He was panting. "Good God, aren't there any police in this part of the city?—I'm going—"

"Wait a minute," Dr. Strang stopped him. "You'll only get yourself into hot water if you go to the police. What can they do?"

She dropped to her knees in the Shanghai street-mind.

"Somebody," the young man said frantically, "must do something!"

"Yes," Dr. Strang agreed. "You will come back to the hotel with us and I will clean and bandage that hole in your head."

"Who could they have been?"

"You must remember, Bill, that Susan is one of the richest women in the world. And that this is China. And that kidnaping for ransom is by no means an uncommon occurrence."

He glanced at Karen when he said this, and she returned his look with cool blue eyes which told him nothing.

"Could you possibly identify any of them?" she asked.

"I could identify one! He was one-eyed. He looked like a spider—dark and bent and twisted. And he wore wooden sandals. They made a clacking sound."

"My dear," Karen said, "China must be teeming with

one-eyed Chinese who wear wooden sandals and look like spiders."

"We'll return to the hotel," her husband grumbled.

He loaded Bill Montgomery into his rickshaw, and walked beside it.

Back in his suite, Dr. Strang washed out the wound in Bill's forehead, painted it with mercurochrome, and pasted absorbent gauze down upon it with adhesive tape. Then he took the dazed young man to his room and told him to go to bed.

"But how about Susan?"

"Don't worry! I'll turn this town inside out to find her, Bill. I'll spend my last dollar, if need be, to find her."

The young man stared at him curiously for a moment, then went into his room.

When Dr. Strang returned, Karen was once again half reclining on the chaise longue, with the jade cigarette holder, empty, in her white, perfect teeth. She was gazing dreamily at the ceiling, with a secret little smile that vanished when her husband came in.

The doctor closed the door and locked it. He began to curse in a low, thick voice. His red-rimmed eyes were blood-shot. Lights struck glints and gleams from them. Nervously, he ran his slender white fingers through his shaggy beard. Then he began beating his fist into the palm of his other hand. He was in a savage mood.

His wife paid no heed.

"WE'VE GOT TO know where that girl was going," the doctor said finally. "We've got to know where Peter Moore is. I did not see how my plans could go wrong. From start to finish, they went completely wrong. It is most mystifying. If you had not been gone so long, sending that damned cable, we would have met her as she went into the rickshaw compound."

"I'm so sorry, Luigi." But she did not look at him. She spoke from afar.

He growled, "I don't understand this kidnaping. How did they know she would be going to the landing stages? It's as if it were neatly arranged. But how could it have been?"

She echoed, "Yes—how could it have been?"

"But we must know where Moore is—we must know! The entire six months past, the plans and dreams of my life—all wasted if we cannot find where that fellow is."

Dr. Strang approached.

The jade lady withdrew her dreamy eyes from the ceiling. The empty cigarette holder gave her a whimsical expression. "Yes, Luigi?"

"Get out that crystal!"

His black, hypnotic eyes were glaring into her opaque, brilliant blue ones.

"No," she whispered. "Oh, please, no!"

He snatched the white jade cigarette holder from her teeth; threw it across the room. "Get that crystal!"

A convulsion of muscles twisted her face, gave it a wry look. Her eyes were large with terror now. "Please, Luigi," she entreated him. "Don't make me! I can't.—You know how it almost destroys me. You know how it simply tears me to pieces. Please don't make me use that crystal!"

He picked up her slender, white wrist in one hand. The other pounced on the back of her slim white neck.

Karen screamed faintly. Even before that sinister hand

touched the back of her head, she was totally changed. Gone entirely was that mask of cool reserve. Gone was all her poise. She was a frightened woman—white and shivering. And when he placed his slender hand at the back of her head, she seemed to collapse.

She moaned, "Luigi! Please, please!"

"Get that crystal!"

"It's in my trunk," with the faintest of whispers.

He left her. She heard him storming about in the bedroom. He returned with a crystal sphere, five or six inches in diameter, resting in a circle of some black, deeply-carved wood. The sphere was clearer than any bubble. It was like a perfectly round ball of clearest atmosphere.

He pulled a small table over and set the sphere, on its wooden base, on the table before Karen.

The golden-haired woman had placed her fingers to her temples. Seated on the edge of the chaise longue, she was slumped down, limp, as if she were exhausted. To her, that sphere was evidently a thing of terror, a thing that inspired in her the utmost dread. Obviously, huddled there, the jade lady was undergoing untold torments of spirit, unguessed agonies of body.

"Read it!" he commanded.

Moaning, she swayed slightly from side to side, pressing her fingers to her temples.

"No, Luigi!—No, please, no! You know how it tears me to pieces."

Again Dr. Strang dropped his dextrous right hand to the back of her neck.

"*Don't!*" she screamed. The lids were half down over his burning black eyes.

With a sigh that was like a ghostly wail, Karen turned and faced the crystal sphere. She dropped her elbows on the edge of the little table and stared down into the transparent, colorless ball.

Every trace of color ebbed from her face. Her body grew tense. Presently it was absolutely rigid. She stared and stared into the crystal sphere, and Dr. Strang, his arms folded on his mighty chest, watched her with wide black eyes.

"Is it beginning to come through?" he growled.

"I can see clouds."

"Work harder!"

"Yes, yes. The clouds are getting thick. They are getting brown. They're mountains. Reddish-brown mountains! They're going—they're moving back! Wait! I can see a river now—a wide brown river. It's racing past. There are boats on the river. Look! There's a steamer!"

"What's the name on it? Catch it—quick!"

"Chang-Sha!"

"Good! The Yangtze-kiang!"

"Yes. The Yangtze-kiang! We're moving up the river—"

"Look for a large town on the left hand bank. Look for twin red pagodas on the riverfront."

"I see them! I see them! Two red pagodas. But we're still moving up the river."

"Past Chung-king?"

"Yes! A day—two days—past."

"No more steamers?"

"No more. Sampans and small junks.—There's another village—on the right bank."

The doctor walked away from her; reached into a box

for a fresh cigar. During that brief moment when his back was turned, Karen looked up from the crystal. Her rigidity relaxed. Her cool, opaque blue eyes sent him an oblique, mysterious glance.

But when he turned about, puffing at the lighted cigar, she was again rigid, again entranced. Again she was chanting.

"A river flows into the Yangtze beside this village, but there is very little water in it. There was once a great deal of water, but now it is almost dry.—We move up that river... I do not know what this means. Something built—and something being built. One is a great concrete dam. Newly built. It rises up out of a deep ravine or cañon.—At the bottom of it, I see, oh, very clearly, a concrete building. Steel poles.—Wires strung along the poles."

"A hydro-electric plant!" Dr. Strang exclaimed.

"Yes! I see names on great, strong crates. The Ling Po Mining Company.—Wait! Now I see a shack, a shanty— one of a group of them sprawling behind the building. There is a man standing there with his hand shading his eyes, looking up at the dam. A slender man with gray eyes, very dark skin—bronzed by the sun. He has a revolver in a holster at his belt. He is wearing a blue flannel shirt, black laced boots—"

"Wait!" the doctor snapped. "We may not need him. You are reading so wonderfully tonight. Quick! Tell me now how we get into Mr. Lu's palace under that lake!"

"I can't! It always goes cloudy when you want me to see that! It's fading now!"

ANGRILY DR. STRANG snatched up the crystal ball. Karen screamed and beat frantically on the table.

She sobbed, "Luigi, I've told you never to do that! You must never snatch it away like that! It hurts! You tear something out of my very heart. How can you be so cruel?"

"Collect yourself, Karen," he said, with a laugh. "You had enough. You did very, very nicely."

She sank back on the chaise longue, seemingly limp, utterly spent. He stood looking down at her. He smiled and took the ball into one of the other rooms.

When he returned, she was still limply lying there. He poured out a drink of whisky and made her take it. But the dullness did not leave her eyes, and her face remained gray. All of the life seemed to have been drained from her by that brief adventure into the occult. She seemed scarcely to be breathing. One hand, under her, was caught to her heart, as if to aid and comfort that disturbed organ.

She did not stir when a knock sounded. Dr. Strang unlocked and opened the door. A tall man with tawny hair was standing in the hall, faintly smiling. His eyes were yellow. His face was long and thin. There was an air of stealth about him. Perhaps it was this that made him somehow resemble a cat—a panther. His large yellow eyes helped. So did his long pointed face.

The yellow eyes looked at the black ones. Dr. Strang put out his slender, effeminate white hand. The newcomer grasped it.

"You're late, Avery," Dr. Strang said.

"My train was delayed in Lang Wen Chow," the other said.

The doctor pulled him into the room and shut the door. "Karen!" he said sharply.

The jade lady lifted herself up.

"Darling," he said, "this is Professor Van Zant—Avery. Avery, this is my wife. Are you surprised to find me married to such a charming, beautiful woman?"

Professor Van Zant picked up Karen's hand and bent over it. He kissed it. His lips were icy cold, wet. They sent a shiver through Karen.

The doctor said, in a kindly tone, "Karen, will you wait in your room while Avery and I have a talk? I am so sorry we must exclude you. You don't mind?"

"Of course not," she said wearily. She gave Professor Van Zant a little smile, went into the rooms beyond and slowly, softly, closed the door behind her.

Once that door was shut, her lassitude, her weariness, vanished. She moved swiftly to the dressing table in her room, switched on the lights, and busied herself with lipstick, rouge and powder. She touched her golden hair here and there with deft fingers. She arched her brows, looked at herself from various angles. She flirted with herself. She smiled archly. She assumed her most demure look. A cloud floated momentarily in the clear surface of her brilliant blue eyes. She sprang up, went to the parlor door and listened.

She heard her husband's deep guttural voice. It came through the wood, a rumbling. Then, on tiptoe, she went through his bedroom and to the door that gave upon the hall. It was locked and bolted. With her slender red lips parted, as if she were breathless with expectancy, she turned the key, shot back the bolt, and let herself out.

8

THE MAN WITH THE JADE BRAIN

PROFESSOR AVERY VAN ZANT was seated on the edge of the chaise longue, his hands clasped over his bony knees. He was a rangy man, giving the effect, even when he half reclined, of alert muscles. Dr. Strang had always called him "the Puma," because he looked like one and acted like one. Professor Van Zant's age was in the neighborhood of forty. He was at present an instructor of psychology in the University of Pekin. His claim to fame lay in a monograph he had written on Mesmer's theory of animal magnetism. He had been Dr. Strang's assistant, or associate, at the San Bernardino sanitarium until it had fallen under the inquisitive scrutiny of local and federal investigators. Since then—for the past six months—he had been in China.

"I am very glad to see you again," Dr. Strang told him, "but there is no time to waste on amenities. Did you turn in your resignation?"

"Immediately. And needless to say I am consumed with curiosity."

The doctor looked at him affectionately. "Avery, I am going to let you in on a very wonderful opportunity. It is a scheme that will take your breath away. Unless I am badly mistaken, you will need hours—days—to digest it. You will be appalled! You will be flabbergasted! Your brain will turn to ice! It makes every other scheme we have ever undertaken ridiculously picayune!"

Professor Van Zant laughed, baring catlike teeth. "Never mind the superlatives," he said. "Give me both barrels, and leave my digestion to me."

The doctor sat down and pulled his chair close, so that he could talk confidentially. Pitching his voice very low, he said, "Have you ever heard of a man named Mr. Lu?"

The yellow eyes flickered. "I associate the name with a Chinese Ambassador to France, many years ago."

Dr. Strang shook his head. "No. It is spelled 'L-u.' I will tell you about him. Mr. Lu is something of a mythological monster. He lives in a castle in the bottom of a lake, away off in the Shan Mountains. Do not look so skeptical, Avery. The facts came to me authoritatively, and I have taken the pains to check them. What I say sounds grossly fantastic, but is sheer truth. You are having trouble with your digestion too soon. I said you would be flabbergasted. This Mr. Lu is a great and mysterious power. He is the greatest power in the Far East. His agents are everywhere. His shadow falls the length of Asia. He is superb! He is magnificent! He is three hundred years old!"

The puma eyes were glowing. "Oh, come, Luigi!"

"I am only telling you what I have gleaned from the most exhaustive investigation. After they drove me out of San Bernardino, I went to Mexico. In Mexico City I met an old Chinese who was an opium addict. We became warm friends. He talked freely. For the first time, I learned that this fabulous Mr. Lu existed. The Chinese call him the Blue Scorpion. I will tell you why in a moment.—Did I mention that I met this charming lady who is my wife in Mexico City? And did I say that she is a gifted occultist—a crystal reader?"

Professor Van Zant laughed softly. "Everything is explained!"

"You are being rude," the doctor reproached him. "She is very beautiful."

"Pardon me, Luigi, but I am much more interested in your mythological monster."

"They call him the Man With the Jade Brain. The story is that three hundred years ago, when Mr. Lu was a very young man, he fell down the face of a cliff. He bounded literally from rock to rock, and when they picked him up at the bottom, he was hardly more than a pulsating pulp. Some surgical genius of the time took him in hand, put him back together—"

"So that he continued to tick?"

"Precisely that. Dozens of bones were broken. His face was destroyed. Part of his brain was so hopelessly mangled that this probably forgotten genius replaced it—"

"Ah, yes! With jade! The Man With the Jade Brain!"

"Perhaps you are right in being so skeptical, Avery."

"Do you expect me to swallow this story—hook, line and sinker? After all, I have a scientific mind."

"The fact remains, my friend, that, whatever Mr. Lu's brain is made of—"

"One moment, Luigi! Does a jade brain think?"

Dr. Strang said impatiently, "Does a silver larynx talk? You and I think we know the processes of human thought. The behaviorist psychologists claim we think with our laryngeal muscles. If we do, then a man with a silver larynx must think with a silver larynx."

Professor Van Zant laughed again. "Don't mind my skepticism. I will concede that your Mr. Lu has a jade brain, and that he does his thinking with it."

"There must be," the doctor said soberly, "a mass of fictitious legend bound up with certain actual facts. But supposing we assume that Mr. Lu is three hundred years old and that he thinks with a jade brain. Whether or not that is true, the fact remains that he is a very great power in the Far East.

"We may also assume—with your permission—that he has found the secret of everlasting life. I would like to know that secret.—And I would like to know other of his secrets."

"Well, why don't you?" Professor Van Zant said lightly.

"Mr. Lu is, without question, the most inaccessible man alive. He lives in this underwater palace, and no one is permitted to see him. So far as I can ascertain, no man has ever looked upon him. And I can tell you why. Vanity! He has no face—nothing but a scar. He is probably a grotesque, a horrible object. He would object to being stared at. My plan is to appeal to his vanity. Nothing more. First, I must get into that underwater palace and talk to him. Once I am there, I shall do nothing but flatter him. I shall impress upon him the wonder of his great age! That's all. Undoubtedly, he is vain of his age. By the way, he speaks all languages."

The yellow eyes were glowing. The professor's head was slowly nodding. "It's a fascinating idea, Luigi."

"You are still laughing at me!" Dr. Strang said testily.

"You think he will refuse to give me an audience! I tell you, he is a genius. Nothing of importance goes on in the world that he does not know about. Why won't he have heard of me?"

"I grant that, Luigi. You are the greatest brain surgeon in America. No one questions that, least of all, I."

"Yes!" the doctor said vigorously. "He will have heard of me. I will be curious to know about his amazing jade brain. My reputation should certainly give me an entrée. You accompany me, of course, as my assistant."

"What is your plan?"

Dr. Strang looked quickly about the room. His eyes rested for a moment on the closed door into the sleeping quarters.

"I have made attempts at getting in touch with him," he said in a guarded voice. "He has ignored them. My only chance is a bold frontal attack. I will find my way into that palace. You, of course, will accompany me. Once there, we will be seized and given an interview with Mr. Lu. We will then depend upon my eloquence."

"It is risky," Avery Van Zant said.

"But it is worth the risk."

"Yes, it is worth the risk, Luigi, but how do we get into this fantastic place?"

"That brings us to our first step. Only one white man has been in that palace—and left it alive. His name is Peter Moore."

"Ah, yes!"

"You've heard of him?"

"Yes. He is rather famous."

"I have just learned that Moore is building a hydro-elec-

tric plant for the Ling Po Mining Company, above Chung
King. He and an American girl named Susan O'Gilvie
visited Lu's underwater palace some months ago. I frightened that information out of the girl only tonight. Mr. Lu
swore her and Moore to secrecy. She has vanished. She
was kidnaped."

"By whom?"

"What difference? Perhaps by Mr. Lu. The fact has been
established that Moore visited his palace. The girl was
blindfolded and saw nothing of value. Moore did, however;
he knows the way. We will find out from him how to get
into the cave of the Blue Scorpion!"

"Suppose he won't talk?"

"I can make any man talk! And when we have the information, we will proceed to Mr. Lu's lake. Now, Avery,
before you start shaking your head in earnest, let me tell
you what it is that I really want from Mr. Lu. I mentioned a
moment ago that Mr. Lu is known as the Blue Scorpion for
a reason. It is because of an amazing, an incredible poison,
of which he alone has the secret.

"My Chinese friend in Mexico City gave me just a
hint. It is some alkaloid, compounded with the venom
taken from an exceedingly poisonous snake found only in
the Tibetan foothills. It is so poisonous—mark this!—so
poisonous that one drop placed in a stream will kill a man
who drinks the water of that stream a mile below!"

Dr. Strang's eyes, in their red rims, were glowing fanat-
ically. His slender white hands were twitching.

"I say," he went on, dropping his voice to a thick whisper,
"that the man who knows the secret of that poison is the

master of the world! I am going to be that man! You are going to share that secret with me!"

He paused, added hastily, "Avery! Death from that poison is so hideous that it staggers the imagination. The victim's body instantly turns a luminous sapphire blue. Its effect is instant and systemic. Yet it peculiarly singles out the brain. The brain turns to water. A few seconds later, the eyes turn as black, as opaque, as two balls of coal! Picture that!"

"And that," Professor Van Zant said, still with his air of mockery, "is why they call Mr. Lu the Blue Scorpion! It's beautiful, Luigi! It's positively poetic!"

"Then you will go with me to see this man Moore?"

A queer light shone in the yellow eyes. "Why do you even ask? Since you put that clever knife of yours into my brain six years ago, have I been capable of refusing any request you have made? Of course I'll go, Luigi!"

9

DELILAH

KAREN STRANG HAD gone to Bill Montgomery's room and softly knocked. When he opened the door, she pushed in past him and closed it. With a bright glance about the room, she turned and looked up into his face. It was haggard and gray. His eyes looked gaunt, and his mouth was bitter. He still wore his tuxedo, but he had removed the collar and tie.

Perhaps it was his woebegone look that drew the soft exclamation of pity from the jade lady. He looked dazed, as if he hardly saw her.

She took his hands and pulled him down beside her on a settee. Then she took his head in her hands and pulled it down to her breast.

"My darling!" she said. "My poor, poor darling!" She held him fiercely. "You mustn't worry, Bill. Everything is going to come out right."

He freed his head from her arms. "Don't do that," Bill Montgomery said.

Karen's smile was indulgent. Her arm was still around his neck. She didn't remove it.

She said tenderly, "You'll never realize how I felt, darling, when I saw you lying there in the road—with that gash in your beautiful forehead!—Oh, Bill! You think I'm horribly bold. But, darling, I've learned that when love comes, one is a fool not to seize it, to hold it fiercely."

Bill Montgomery got up. His dazed look was gone. He was plainly uncomfortable, embarrassed—and angry.

"Karen, you know I'm in love with Susan."

"I know. I've seen that kind of love. It's infatuation. Besides, she doesn't care at all for you. There never has been and never will be any other man for that girl but Peter Moore. You might just as well get over it now. You are much too impulsive. You need a woman of experience. The woman you need, darling, is me."

"Please, Karen—"

"Are you thinking of that bearded monster? You know I loathe him, Bill. If you wish, you may think that I married him to escape boredom. That's close enough to the real reason."

The young man stared at her. "I don't see how you can be so damned cool!" he said angrily. "What state do you suppose I'm in? I don't even know what you're saying. What are those devils doing with Susan?—Where is she? Where did they take her?"

"Don't worry about her. She's all right, darling. I can assure you."

"How can you assure me?" he cried.

Karen smiled gently. "But I am assuring you, Bill. Nothing has happened to her. She is in safe hands."

"You don't know that!"

"I'm wiser than you think, Bill."

Bill Montgomery folded his arms on his chest and

looked down at her menacingly. "What do you mean by that?" he growled.

"Just what I say, darling. I know that the girl is in safe hands, and I know that nothing will happen to her."

He stared down at her a moment longer. "Stop beating about the bush!" he snapped. "Tell me what you know, or, by heaven—!"

Karen sprang up. The warmth was gone from her eyes. They were coolly, opaquely blue once more.

"You wouldn't hurt me!" she whispered.

"Tell me," he said grimly, "what you know!"

The jade lady shrugged. "But haven't you guessed? Don't you know what a powerful man Peter Moore is in China?"

"You mean," Bill gasped, "he staged that kidnaping?"

"Of course, dear!"

"Damn him!—Where is he?"

"Darling, forget that girl. I am very wise. I know. Peter Moore is two thousand miles away—several days' travel beyond the most westerly navigable part of the Yangtze Kiang. He's building a hydro-electric plant up there. It's one of the most difficult and dangerous spots in the world to reach. Rapids. Whirlpools. Unfriendly natives."

Bill said savagely, "Do you mean to say that Peter Moore, two thousand miles away, had Susan kidnaped?"

"I mean exactly that."

"But it's incredible!"

"You don't know China," she said, sighing. Her eyes were mysterious. "So," she went on, "you see how foolish it is for you to remain infatuated with that girl."

"If she's so madly in love with him," Bill said, "why did he have to kidnap her?"

"I'll tell you why," Karen said grimly. "She has not seen him in months. She has been trying to get over her infatuation. He was afraid she would."

"Did she tell you so?"

"Yes, dear.—Now, I must go back. The monster will be wondering where I am. Good night!" She reached up quickly and kissed him. "Stop worrying!"

She let herself out and returned to her room, bolting and locking the door of her husband's bedroom after her. She seated herself again at her dressing table. She looked at herself.

"Oh, Bill!" she murmured to the sleek, golden-haired, blue-eyed image in the mirror. "My poor, poor darling! It was necessary. I had no choice." Her lips remained parted. She tilted her head a little. "Karen, you are so beautiful," she whispered. "You are so much lovelier!"

Her face hardened. Fiercely, she whispered, "Damn her!—Damn her little soul!"

The blue eyes grew more brilliant. Tears filled the under lids, welled out, coursed down her cheeks. The jade lady softly sniffled. Anguish softened her face, and she saw this softness softened even more by the blur of tears. She dropped her head suddenly upon her arms and began to sob.

Some time later, when the parlor door opened and her husband came into her room, she was still huddled there, with her golden head on her arms. But she was quiet now. She was limp.

He said, "Ah! Do you still feel badly, Karen?"

And she answered faintly, "I wish I were dead!"

BILL MONTGOMERY WAS packing. Blindly, in a frenzy

of haste, he was jamming things into traveling bags. He had changed to a dark gray suit, in the hip pocket of which he placed a loaded automatic pistol. From time to time he took the pistol out and looked at it. At such times there was about his mouth an expression of grim satisfaction.

10

RAGGED COOLIE

THE OUTLINE OF the cañon's rim was slowly being blurred by the dusk, as if successive layers of gray gossamer were being drawn over it. Above it, in the darkly opalescent sky, lavender clouds were as delicate as blown glass. The afterglow had faded. The last diffusion of daylight transformed the little river into a flat ribbon of lead.

Peter Moore was seated on a camp stool outside his shack, with the bit of an empty pipe between his teeth, his eyes on the river. His thoughts were as dark as the darkest rock-shadows below him, and quite as heavy as the metal of which the river seemed to be composed. Seven days remained to him in which to finish this job, and he did not see how he could possibly accomplish it.

What had started off as a pleasant and profitable adventure had degenerated to a source of endless worries. Each day brought its toll of frustrations; things that went wrong; things that vanished. Today it had been a box of pilot bulbs for the switchboard in the control room. Yesterday it had been a kilovolt meter and a synchronoscope. If it wasn't a drum of some special kind of lubricating oil, it would be a carton of cotter pins, or a case of waterproof paint. Little things. Each of them, taken by itself, wasn't important.

But a modern hydro-electric plant consists of a million of such trivial things.

No matter how close a guard Moore set over the operations, things mysteriously disappeared, things mysteriously went wrong. And he could not believe that Mr. Lu was at the bottom of these annoyances, these petty frustrations. Mr. Lu never concerned himself with such trivialities.

But whatever their source, Peter Moore was determined that, one week from today, sixty thousand volts should surge through these wires. Rains, back in the mountains, had filled the impounding lake. One week from today he would, Moore grimly told himself, give the order to the crew to open the wicket gates. He wanted the pleasure of standing at the board in the control room and of sending thirteen thousand volts into the buss-yard!

WHEN THAT MIRACLE was accomplished, Peter Moore intended to take a well-earned vacation. He was going to saddle a horse, load a pack animal with provisions, and go off on a week of exploration, purely for the fun of it. He wanted to investigate, among other things, a certain pagoda that Lee Gow, one of his assistants who would eventually be put in charge of maintenance, had reported seeing in a valley some thirty odd miles to the north.

A *charcoal* pagoda! That was how Lee Gow had somewhat mystically described it. A black pagoda, lost in the hills; relic of a forgotten era of Chinese civilization. As black as midnight, it nestled there amid tall and gloomy cedars. There was no other structure, no habitation of any kind, within miles of this lonesome pagoda. Why was it there? Who had built it in that secluded spot? Why was it black?

And why its amazing legend, which made the natives treat it like a place accursed? The legend was that the charcoal pagoda was tenanted by a white dragon—a reptile forty feet in length with green fire eyes and a foul steaming breath.

Peter Moore had seen "dragons" and other legendary monsters of that type become nothing more frightful than stray lions, tigers—or nothing at all! After months of dreary labor spent in building a hydro-electric plant, it would be an amusing adventure to come to grips with a forty-foot dragon that breathed steam and lighted its way with green fire eyes.

He was wondering in which box his rifle was packed, when his eyes detected a dim fluttering along the extreme lower edge of his vision. He centered them where the fluttering had seemed to occur. What he had seen had, perhaps, been a bird. The light was almost gone. He could no longer see the leaden shimmer of sky on water. Lights glowed feebly at the windows of the other shacks. A light, cool breeze carried cooking odors to him.

Dimly, very dimly, against the slate gray of dusk, he saw that object move again. To the left of it the great white bulk of the power house loomed like a block of chalk in the gathering darkness. He suspected that it was someone who had no right to be prowling about down there.

Moore slipped into the shack for his revolver. He snapped open the cylinder, to make sure that it was loaded, and went outside again. Moving stealthily down the path, he saw a gray shape move against the deeper gray of dusk. Then he heard a faint gasp and the rattle of dislodged stones. Waiting a moment, he heard the stones splash into the river.

Moore was now close enough to make out the ghostly figure of a short, thin coolie—a coolie in rags. He had seen the rags flutter.

Endeavoring to make no sound, the American swiftly descended the steep path.

The coolie had stopped, and was evidently looking through one of the windows into the power plant. His silhouette against the white wall made him an excellent target.

Moore, wondering if this coolie was responsible for the mysterious disappearance of tools and parts, was strongly tempted to shoot—and to ask questions afterward. But he refrained. Stealthily, he covered the remaining distance.

In the interval that had elapsed since he first saw the fluttering rags the stars had come out, and their faint, cool light somewhat diminished the gray gloom. As the coolie, on tiptoe, strained up and peered into the dark building, Moore shoved the muzzle of the revolver none too gently into the trespasser's ribs.

There was a terrified gasp, followed by a sharp little scream. The coolie spun about. In the dim light of the stars, Moore saw a small, gaunt, white face and two large dark eyes.

The coolie said, in a girl's voice, "Peter!—Oh, darling!"

Thin, cold arms flew about his neck and fiercely clung.

He said, in an explosion of incredulity, "Oh, no!—Susan! Oh, no!"

SHE WAS, IN his arms, hardly more than bones. She was shivering. Her teeth were chattering. Now, from sheer relief, she began to cry. He tried to console her, but he was so bewildered by this unexpected visitation that he, too, was all but incoherent.

He had thought she was in Japan, perhaps Manila. And it was incredible to him that Susan could be in rags—the ragged, tattered clothing of a river coolie. Susan, perhaps the richest girl in America! Susan, with her beautiful, smart, sophisticated clothes; with her jewels which were, in themselves, a treasure! And—Susan in tattered rags! Susan, so thin, so gaunt, he hardly recognized her!

"I'm f-f-freezing!"

The air wasn't very cold. He supposed she must be having a chill from exposure, exhaustion, starvation. He picked her up in his arms, and carried her up the path to his shack. From her faintly gasped exclamation, between the tremors of her chill, he gathered that he had positively no idea how delighted she was to find him at last. After all these weeks!

"I can't help bawling. You don't know what a relief it is!"

Nothing in his life had ever shocked him so much as this.

"Peter! You're glad to see me!"

"I'm overwhelmed!" Why, she couldn't weigh more than eighty-five pounds! No procession of authentic ghosts could ever have astonished him so much as this starved little apparition in his arms.

He kicked open the door of the shack; and supporting Susan with one arm, found matches and lit candles. He yanked a blanket off his bunk and folded her up in it. Then he sat her on the bunk and busied himself at the little tin stove. It had originally been a five-gallon gasoline can. A hole in front and another at the top sufficed for the introduction of fuel and air. The chimney was of clay and Portland cement, and was as hard as brick.

When the stove was roaring and sending out waves of heat, Moore got up from his knees, to find that Susan had fallen over on the bunk, asleep. He arranged her in a more comfortable position and covered her with blankets to the chin.

For a few minutes, in the candle light, he squatted down and studied her thin, white little face. He was, he was forced to admit, delighted to see Susan again—even a Susan who was so thin, so starved, so ragged. But her presence, unless he was mistaken, meant trouble.

He suspected that Susan, with her love of thrills, her propensity for getting herself into difficulties, had upset another apple cart.

She invariably sought trouble—and found it!—as unerringly as a ferret seeks a holed-up rabbit. She disproved, time after time, that a burned child dreads the flame. Her thirst for adventure was, in itself, a fire that no amount of terrifying experience could quench.

Cold reason told Moore this. Susan never came to him unless she was in hot water—or preparing to pull him into hot water. Her present emaciated condition indicated that she was in more serious trouble than usual. He wondered anxiously what she had done. And he had a ghastly premonition that it had some connection with the Blue Scorpion.

PETER, WONDERING, SET about getting her something to eat. His Chinese servant was doing sentinel duty on the dam tonight; had gone on watch immediately after serving Moore's supper. He rummaged about the shelves, finding cans of tomatoes, sardines, soup, beans and a tin of freshly opened biscuits. He opened cans, and placed them on the stove to heat. He made coffee.

He discovered presently that the heat was waking Susan up. Her eyes, under their long black lashes, were lazily watching him.

Moore walked over and looked down at her. She smiled. There was warm color in her face now. She wriggled about under the blankets and gazed up at him starily. He knew that look. It confirmed his apprehensions. Susan was contrite. That meant that Susan, at the opportune moment, was going to explain in exciting detail that it really wasn't her fault, but that she had been the victim of irresistible circumstances.

"You little devil!" he growled.

Susan sat up with the urgency of a Jack-in-the-box.

"Darling," she wailed, "if you'll just listen—"

"Wait till after you've eaten."

She meekly nodded. "It's a harrowing story," she said.

"It always is," the man said dryly.

"The most horrible man—" she began again.

"Eat first," he stopped her. "Talk afterward."

"Yes, Peter.—Isn't this place cozy? It's just like a box car, isn't it? Only it isn't on wheels. You're just a Spartan, aren't you?—What am I eating? I'm starved, darling!"

He placed steaming soup before her on a table which his Chinese boy had fashioned with loving care from a packing case. Susan devoured all the soup, all the tomatoes, all the sardines, all the biscuits, and most of a can of warmed-up corned beef. It was, she said, the first civilized food she had tasted in almost two months—since leaving

Shanghai. She had been living on coolie rice and river fish and boiled weeds. It had been simply too hideous.

"I'll never look another grain of rice in the eye without shuddering."

If she hadn't had courage, she might have eaten slowly, to postpone the hour of reckoning. But Susan never lacked courage. She could have got along with a great deal less courage.

Peter, watching her, was torn between an almost overwhelming pity and mirth. She ate so ravenously. She was so pathetically thin. And she looked so jaunty, so debonair, perched there on the edge of the bunk, in the torn and tattered garments of a river coolie.

But her violet eyes were bright and her cheeks were pink from the heat and the excitement of seeing him again. He often disapproved of Susan's trouble-hunting nature, but he knew he could not have tolerated a life in which there was no Susan.

When she had finished the coffee and smoked a cigarette, she said, "Now, come over here and sit beside me, because if you don't sit here and hold my hand, I'm afraid I won't have the strength to tell you about it."

He moved the table back and seated himself beside her.

Looking up at him with glowing, excited eyes, she said, "I'm so glad to see you again that I could positively bawl.— You haven't kissed me! That one down the hill didn't count. I was too numb."

He kissed her. Susan's face was feverish. She said her stomach was apt to give her a temperature from the sheer excitement of receiving so much food all at once.

"IT'S BEEN PERFECTLY hideous," she said. "It's been like a nightmare. I was kidnaped in Shanghai. I escaped when they tried to tie my hands and feet and throw me into a sampan. I stowed away on a fishing junk that was going up-river under sail. An old woman found me hiding in the stern and stole all my clothes and gave me these in return. I was dead broke. I had to beg my way. I slept in abandoned rice mills, in fields. I must have walked hundreds of miles, and I never stirred except at night. My feet are so calloused I could walk on spikes and not feel it!...

"It was raining almost all the time. I caught a horrible cold near Cheman-Foo, and was so sick I thought I'd die. I learned to beg from young women, not the old ones. The old ones were always mean. One of them threw a stone at me. I memorized the names of all the people I could who were kind to me. Tomorrow, before I forget them, I must write them down, so I can send them presents. Even now, Peter, it doesn't seem possible that it could have been I who went through such ghastly experiences....

"But I had to reach you. I didn't dare go to consuls—I didn't dare go near civilized places for fear they'd be watching for me and get me again."

"Let's begin a little nearer the beginning," Peter suggested. "Who kidnaped you?"

"I haven't the faintest idea!"

Peter's hopes were fading. He said, "Reassure me on just one point, Susan. Tell me you haven't mentioned our visit to Mr. Lu to any one!"

"But I did, darling!" she wailed. "It was positively bullied out of me!"

Peter looked at her eyes with a feeling that was, curiously, merely one of disappointment. There was only one

word for this—betrayal. Susan's thirst for excitement had
drawn him into many dangerous predicaments. But this
time she had betrayed him; for he had exacted the most
solemn promise from her, when they parted, that she would
mention that fantastic visit to no one.

11

THE DISAPPEARANCE

PETER FOLDED HIS arms on his chest and said quietly, "I understand."

Susan, sensing his attitude, cried, "Darling! You know I wouldn't do such a thing deliberately! I tell you I was bullied. A man named Dr. Strang bullied the secret of the Blue Scorpion out of me. At dinner, on my last night in Shanghai. I was having dinner with him and his wife and another American—a Bill Montgomery—in the doctor's suite, and he began to abuse you. He said the most outrageous things about you. He made me so furious I could have murdered him. He said you were—"

"It doesn't matter," Peter stopped her. "Is this man's full name Luigi Strang?"

"Yes!" Susan cried. "Do you know him?"

Peter said quietly, "That explains everything. Do you know just who Dr. Luigi Strang is?"

"He had a sanitarium for what he called 'brain cases,' just outside San Bernardino, California. He's on his honeymoon—with a very blond bride. He's a horrible, shaggy monster. That's all I know.—I could kill him!" Susan panted. "What do you know about him?"

"I heard sometime ago that he was headed for China,"

Peter answered. "He was once a famous brain surgeon—
one of the greatest brain surgeons in the world. Then his
own brain went wrong. He opened that California sanitarium and filled it with mental cases. He operated on
the brains of these patients—I don't know how many, but
a great many. He would cut out a small lobe, or an area,
which made his victims, in some strange way, completely
enslaved to him. What caused the authorities to investigate him was the fact that his patients invariably willed
him every dollar they had. It was nothing but a horrible,
cold-blooded racket. Now, tell me just what happened."

Susan told him, graphically and in detail, of the events
of that evening, beginning with the cocktail party at the
French Consulate, and did not slight her terrifying experiences in Chinese City. Peter asked her numerous questions.
Where had she met Bill Montgomery? Where had she met
the Strangs? Who had introduced them to her? Who had
Mrs. Strang been before she married Dr. Strang? What
had Dr. Strang given Susan to drink before that dinner?
On one point he was particularly interested—the one-eyed
spider-like coolie who wore wooden sandals.

"Are you quite sure he was the same one who followed
you in Chinese City, and who headed the gang of kidnap-
ers?"

Susan was positive. What puzzled Peter was the
one-eyed coolie's apparent knowledge that Susan would
leave the hotel hurriedly and would go down to the landing stages some time that evening.

"He was waiting there for you. How did he know you
would be down there? I mean, who tipped him off? I think
he is one of Mr. Lu's men, but could it be that Dr. Strang

*Leading the intruders was one whose
eyes were hypnotically black.*

is one of Mr. Lu's men? Did Mr. Lu have Dr. Strang force
you to make that admission as a test?—Yet that doesn't
sound like the Blue Scorpion.—And just where does this
Mongomery lad fit in?"

SUSAN WAS SURE that Bill Montgomery was perfectly
innocent. Peter wasn't sure that any one in any way
connected with the business was above suspicion.

"Bill Montgomery's nothing but a handsome, hopeless
romantic," Susan murmured.

"Hopelessly in love with you," said Peter.

"Jealous?"

"Not unless you're in love with him," Peter said. "Are
you?"

"The trouble with me," Susan said, "is that I can't see any
other man in the world but you.—I'm hopeless."

"And the trouble with me," Peter said, "is that I'm in love
with a girl who is worth umpteen-billion dollars—and my
pride simply burns me up."

"False pride!"

"Oh, sure.—But I'll make my million yet."

"Ah, yes!" Susan said airily. "Won't we have the dandiest times going about the world in our wheel chairs?"

He didn't like that. "I may surprise you.—This deal, if somebody doesn't throw a monkey wrench into it, will give me a good running start." He sighed. "Susan, I never realized how much a million dollars was."

Any reference to Susan's wealth and Peter's poverty always infuriated Susan. And her happiness at seeing him again was too great to permit fury to spoil it. She asked him about the job, and he discussed it enthusiastically and in detail, neglecting to mention the mysterious troubles he'd been having.

"You'll be here," he said, "when we turn the power on—a week from today. That's what the contract calls for. In fact, I'll let you turn the power on. I'll arrange now for a place for you to bunk. You can double with the wife of my maintenance man. She's a charming, very modern young Chinese woman. You'll like Mrs. Lee Gow. She's a great cook, and neater than pins. Her husband can bunk up here with me. Mrs. Lee will fix you up with clothes. She's about your size. And for a while you'll do nothing but eat and sleep."

Susan was looking at him broodingly. "You don't seem to be expecting trouble from Mr. Lu."

Peter said quickly, "Oh, no. We'll be back in Shanghai too soon for that."

He was, of course, lying to prevent her from worrying. He knew that there was no way to escape trouble with Mr. Lu. It was useless, trying to escape to the coast now.

Whatever Mr. Lu wished to do, to repay them for betraying his trust, he would do. They were completely at his mercy.

What form would Mr. Lu's vengeance take? Some fantastic, horrible punishment? Peter Moore had heard of the punishment which the Blue Scorpion meted out to one pair of lovers. The man had been buried alive, so that only his head was above ground. And the girl had been horribly tortured to death before her fiancé's eyes. He was left there—with her body, broken and torn, lying a few feet from his eyes—until he died of thirst and starvation.

But Susan knew nothing of such legends.

SUSAN LIKED MRS. Lee Gow tremendously, and was infatuated with the Lees' three-months-old daughter, who resembled nothing in the world but a bright-eyed laughing Chinese doll. Mrs. Lee supplied Susan with Chinese clothing from her own wardrobe, and undertook to nurse her back to health. Susan wasn't actually ill, but undernourishment and hardships had weakened her. Under Mrs. Lee's care, Susan immediately began to recover her weight and her appearance. Her cheeks lost their hollows and regained their color. Her body quickly lost its pathetic thinness. Before the week drew to an end, it seemed to Peter that she was as lovely and as energetic as she had ever been.

The trouble was that after a very few days Susan was too vigorous to do nothing but eat and rest. She began to explore the power house, the buss-yard. And soon the great concrete wall of the dam was tempting her. She wanted to climb to the top and see the lake, wanted to look down inside the penstock and see the eighty-ton steel gate which Peter had installed there. It would serve in case of emergency, to protect the turbines and the wicket gates which were so cleverly built into the turbine housings.

Late one afternoon, with a small automatic pistol in a holster at her waist, she made the climb up the zigzag rock path to the top of the dam.

Peter, in the buss-yard, saw her slim, erect figure silhouetted against the late afternoon sky as she walked along the dam and the lip of the spillway. Watching her, he smiled. She was so valiant, so damned inquisitive, so jaunty. There was no one in the world, he reflected, quite like Susan!

PERHAPS IT WAS half an hour later that he heard what might have been the faint echo of the riveting machine across the yard. But the riveting machine had been silent for several minutes. Again, faint, but clear and sharp, he heard the staccato rattling. In all, there were six distinct detonations. Then he recalled that there were just six bullets in the pistol which he had insisted that Susan carry.

He ran, climbed and clawed his way up the path to the top of the dam. He looked frantically about. The lake was calm and innocently blue. The hills were glamorously blue and purple in the misty dusk.

There was no sign of Susan. He ran across the dam to the other side. There he found three dead men—bronzed and powerful hillmen they had been in life. These three Susan had evidently accounted for. Peter suddenly sat down on a rock, with a sickening, overwhelming sense of defeat. There was no question in his mind that Mr. Lu had struck. His men had been waiting, perhaps days, for this very opportunity. Unquestionably, too, strong, fresh, fast horses had been held in waiting. They rode like the wind, these hillmen. Pursuit was out of the question.

Where, Peter wondered, was the Chinese sentry? Day and night, he had kept a man guarding the dam.

He found the body of the sentry a hundred feet away, near the edge of the lake, tumbled down into a pile of bowlders. His throat had been slit.

Sick and weary, Peter returned to his shack. There was nothing for him to do but go to the Lake of the Flying Dragon. It would be impossible to save Susan from whatever fate Mr. Lu had in store for her, he knew, but he could not abandon her to that fate.

He could not leave, however, until he had pulled himself together. He would have Mrs. Lee Gow make him some strong coffee, then he would saddle a horse and start.

Heavy footfalls sounded in the path as he started for the door. Through the little window, he glimpsed a man plunging up the path—a tall young man, hatless, with curly black hair and a darkly flushed, handsome face.

That glimpse was sufficient to apprise Peter Moore that his urgent visitor must surely be the handsome young American cattle prince whom Susan had known in Shanghai. There was a black revolver in Bill Montgomery's right hand.

12

VISITORS

THE AMERICAN CATTLE prince charged the door of Peter's shack and kicked it open. He entered the shack with all the power, all the ferocity of a charging tiger. His rush carried him half across the room.

It took his eyes some moments to grow used to the darkness inside the shack. Then, with the revolver at his hip, he bore down on the dim, slender figure beside the window.

Bill Montgomery was panting from an excess of emotion and energetic determination. He reminded Peter of some mythical young god of vengeance.

"You dirty fortune hunter!" he panted. "Where is she?"

"Put that gun away!"

"Damn you!—I'll blow your brains out if you don't tell me where that girl is! She's here!—I know she's here!"

Peter, regarding him, would have been amused, had it not been for the feeling of tragic futility which had overcome him since Susan's disappearance. Susan had told him how Bill Montgomery dramatized his every emotion. There was no question that he saw himself now as the American hero rescuing the girl he loved from the hands of a black-hearted villain.

The black-hearted villain, who was Peter Moore, said:

"Bill, you're just one hour too late. Miss O'Gilvie has just been kidnaped."

"Hah!" Bill said, sneering. "Do you expect me to believe that? I'm here to get her, and I'm going to get her! Tell me where she is, or, by God, I'll drill you!"

Peter walked slowly toward him, with arms folded on chest. It was a trick, often useful with such impulsive and inexperienced young men as Bill Montgomery.

The cattle prince raised the muzzle of the weapon with the obvious intention of pulling the trigger. One second later, he was unarmed, and the revolver was a dark glitter, flying toward a corner of the shack.

"Now," Peter began quietly, "if you'll let me explain—"

A large brown fist, landing fair and square on his left cheekbone, ended that peaceable suggestion. It was evident that the cattle prince had a few surprises of his own.

As Peter staggered back against the wall, almost out on his feet, the belligerent young man from Montana panted, "I'm going to teach you a lesson that you'll never forget! I'm going to beat you to a pulp. Oh, I've heard all about you—you dirty, lying, four-flushing, cheap crook!"

While Peter Moore, backed against the wall, was recovering from the jarring effects of that punch, the man from Montana embroidered his theme. He had grown up with cowboys and he had a splendid vocabulary.

Peter learned, roughly, that he was low enough to steal the pennies from a dead man's eyes; that he was nothing but a cheap bum, a bluff, a braggart, a beach comber. He made no attempt to justify himself. When the fury of this human volcano had run its course, he would explain. He did not altogether blame Bill Montgomery for this savage attitude. Bill didn't understand, that was all. In due course Peter would make everything clear.

But it was destined not to be so simple as that. Fairly in mid breath, the cattle prince followed up one of the unkindest of his denunciations with his large and expert fists.

Peter's fists, while not so large, were fairly expert, too. Often he had been compelled to rely on their skill and readiness in unavoidable brawls, from Rangoon to Mukden. Peter's nature was peaceful. He disliked fighting. But he knew how.

IN THE GATHERING dusk, the fight began. It should have been very onesided, because the man from Montana was almost a head taller than Peter; his power was ox-like, and obviously he had been scientifically trained in the use of his fists. But it wasn't as one-sided as it should have been, for Peter was faster.

The gloom of falling night was in his favor; it made him a phantom. In the first flurry of blows he came off unscratched, but sent a savage punch to Bill's jaw which sent the man from Montana staggering out of the door and several feet down the path.

With silent fury, the avenger returned. Peter sidestepped his rush, and Bill Montgomery, unable to check his own attack, smashed into the cold stove and sent it rolling and banging into a corner. He returned. Peter slipped away from him again; jumped back and dealt the man from Montana another savage punch in the jaw.

That one set Bill off balance. He fell against the improvised shelves of provisions. Frantically he tried to maintain his balance, clawed at the shelves and brought them down about him in a tumbling debris of canned goods. Another man would have used these heavy cans as weapons. A can of corned beef is a missile not to be scorned. But Bill was a clean fighter. All the fighting he knew he had evidently learned in a ring. Possibly he had been on a college boxing team.

So, returning to the fray, he used nothing but his fists. He landed a punch in Peter's stomach. Peter fought himself into a clinch, and resisted the temptation to kick Bill Montgomery in the shins. He wanted, and would eventually have, Bill's friendship. And it mustn't be marred by a later recollection, on Bill's part, that unclean tactics had been employed.

Bill punched him cleanly out of the clinch, and followed his advantage with a swinging blow to the face, which missed. Peter's next clean punch sent Bill Montgomery crashing against the built-in bunk. He rebounded, and launched furious rights and lefts; but where Peter had been he now was not.

The fury of the Montana man was wearing him out, but he would not stop. Peter began to have a deeper and deeper liking for Bill Montgomery. The cattleman had, practically, whipped himself by his own magnificent wrath; but he would not admit that he was whipped.

Peter knocked him down four times in thirty seconds. Each time, it took Bill longer to get to his feet, and he was more uncertain.

The fourth time, Peter said, "Listen, Bill. Let's cut this out. You've got me all wrong."

"I'll not quit," Bill wheezed, "until you're unconscious."

It was almost dark now—so murky that all details of the interior of the shack were lost in the purple blur. Almost sobbing, Bill threw himself again at the phantom.

Once more Peter knocked him down. He hated to do it. But there was no choice. If this fight had been conducted in a ring, even the cruelest of referees would have stopped it long ago.

Eventually, Peter stopped it by knocking Bill Montgomery completely out. The man from Montana fell—and did not rise. And when Peter spoke his name, Bill did not answer.

THEN PETER FOUND matches, and eventually found candles among the debris on the floor. He lighted candles and lifted the unconscious warrior into the bunk.

The shack, to judge from appearances, might have been visited by a particularly ferocious twister. Not a single shelf remained on any wall; the stove was smashed; the table was in splinters; the makeshift chairs were smashed; the floor was littered with blueprints, drawing instruments, cans of provisions, tobacco, broken pipes, clothing, and fragments of wood.

Peter glanced at himself in the fragment of a mirror that he had tacked on a wall. His jaw, on the left side, was swollen and discolored, but otherwise he was clean of marks.

Unfortunately, Bill Montgomery was not in such good shape. His nose was red and swollen; it might be broken. The skin about both eyes already showed indications of discoloring. His lips were puffed.

Peter, deliberating upon what to do about Bill, decided to leave him a brief note, saying that he was sorry, but that it was true that Susan had disappeared, and that he was going in search of her. Unless he was mistaken, Bill would probably start fighting again the moment he recovered consciousness; he would not believe a word that Peter told him.

Peter was rummaging about among the litter on the floor for a pencil that was unbroken when he heard foot-falls on the path. However, he paid no attention to them, thinking that Lee Gow was dropping in to inquire about Susan's prolonged absence.

A sense of utter futility flowed over him again. He had planned to send the first water through the turbines tomor-row afternoon. And he had looked forward to the pleasure it would give Susan to be the one to switch the high volt-age onto the lines. He did not care now whether or not the current ever surged on those laboriously erected lines. He would say nothing to Lee Gow or any one else about his plans. He would simply go to Mr. Lu single-handed.

Some one thumped on the closed door of the shack.

Now, there are thumps and thumps. This one was of the important variety. Certainly, it was not the discreet tapping of Lee Gow or of any of the other young Chinese engi-neers or foremen. Only a white man would thump with such assurance, such arrogance.

Peter opened the door and stared in surprise at a group of faces lighted dimly orange by the candles. Two of these were white men. Ranged behind them were a dozen tall, strange Chinese. Darkly bronzed men these were, of the kind that Peter had found dead at the top of the dam. And there was no question in his mind who one of the white men was. Susan's description of the man made him easier to identify than Bill Montgomery. Black—hypnotically black—red-rimmed eyes; shaggy brown beard; wet red lips.

A deep, powerful voice said:

"I am Dr. Luigi Strang."

13

A PROPOSITION

PETER SHIFTED HIS eyes from the face of the one-time celebrated brain surgeon to the eyes of the doctor's companion. Fascinating eyes, these. As yellow as any jungle cat's. And they were not quite human. Some quality was missing from them. Peter did not know then that this same quality of something missing was characteristic of the eyes of every man or woman upon whom Dr. Luigi Strang had performed his notorious brain operation. All Peter knew was that the doctor's companion, because of the quality which was missing in those yellow eyes, set in the slender, yellowish face, gave this man the look of a puma.

"This is my associate, Professor Van Zant. We should like to come in and have a little chat with you, Mr. Moore."

Peter, glancing at the bronzed, grim faces of the Chinese guards, said irritably, "I'm just leaving on an important errand. I haven't time for a chat."

The brain specialist smiled. "Just a moment, Moore. Perhaps I can relieve your mind of certain misapprehensions. Were you about to start on a hunt for Miss O'Gilvie?"

Peter felt a thrill of antagonism run along his muscles. He felt an instant and tremendous disliking for these two scientists. He would not have needed Susan's biased account of her dealings with Dr. Strang to have arrived at this dislike. It was the mutual hostility that is aroused when two entirely different natures meet, and by their very unlikeness strike sparks of mutual antagonism. It would have occurred under any circumstances, any conditions— instantaneous, full-fledged hatred.

When Peter, hostile and suspicious, merely stared at him, Dr. Strang said jocularly, "You need have no fears, Mr. Moore. Miss O'Gilvie is, at this moment, safe with my wife.—Where she is, of course, is a matter that I am not prepared at this moment to divulge."

Peter did not betray his relief. At that moment he felt that any fate was preferable to Susan's falling into the hands of the Blue Scorpion.

It was obvious to him that Dr. Strang and Professor Van Zant were men with an ax—perhaps more than one ax—to grind. He had suspected, when listening to Susan's excited account of her adventures, that Dr. Strang wanted, among other things, to know his, Peter's, whereabouts.— The doctor was, then, simply a man with a proposition; and he was ready to back up that proposition with his native guards and the threat of what might happen to Susan if it was not accepted.

There was no proposition he could make that Peter could not handle with agility. Peter was absolutely sure of this. Somehow the proposition would concern Mr. Lu. Of that he was quite as certain.

Peter smiled somewhat grimly. Glancing from the yellow eyes to the black ones, he said, "So this is nothing but a social call? By all means, come in, gentlemen! I must apologize not only for the simplicity of my quarters, but for the condition they are in. I have just had another visitor—who was less subtle."

PETER, BACKING AWAY, watched the shaggy face of the brain specialist as the two men cautiously came in. They seemed wary. Dr. Strang, looking quickly over the topsy-turvy scene, was the first to discover Bill Montgomeny lying on the bunk.

He walked over and looked down into his face. Then he turned and said, "I knew he was coming to Chung-King by the steamer that followed ours up the river; but I didn't think he'd make such good time in from Chennan-Fou. I see that you used violence."

Peter Moore, smiling thinly, said, "I'm sorry I can't offer you chairs, gentlemen."

"This fellow," the doctor rumbled, more to himself than to Peter, "is a damned nuisance." He was referring, Peter knew, to Bill Montgomery. A faint snore from the recumbent young man indicated that he had slipped easily from unconsciousness into sleep.

"I must warn you, Mr. Moore," Dr. Strang said, "that it is useless for you to attempt violence with us. These men are armed; they are fully instructed. Besides, I want you to know that my own intentions are absolutely friendly."

"I gathered that," Peter said dryly, and found the cold yellow eyes of "the puma man" resentfully regarding him.

"Shut that door," Dr. Strang said.

Professor Van Zant shut the door, and folding his arms, stood with his back against it. "Before we go any further," he said, "I'd feel more comfortable if Moore disarmed himself."

Peter hesitated, and said, "Certainly, gentlemen. You'll find me the soul of coöperation." He tossed his revolver on the bunk at the feet of the sleeping cattle prince.

Dr. Strang briskly rubbed his hands together. He said, "Nothing is to be gained by beating about the bush. We come here, Moore, with a proposition that may strike you as amazing, even fantastic. I am sure it is the most amazing proposition that ever came your way. But before stating it, I will first tell you what your contribution must be. I want you to accompany me to Mr. Lu's palace. I know that if I go there with you, he will give me an audience."

"I guessed that was what you wanted of me," said Peter.

"Very well. You perhaps know who I am. I am the greatest brain surgeon in the world. My fame is international—world-wide.—Now, you have talked with this so-called Blue Scorpion. You know that he is a man of amazing learning. You also know that no important event transpires in the world without his hearing of it. In short, you will, of course, assume that he has heard of me." Strang hesitated.

Peter nodded. He was amazed by nothing, least of all by this madman's conceit.

Dr. Strang glared. "You grant that?"

"Oh, yes. There's no doubt about it."

"Very well. Mr. Lu, being so vastly erudite, would be actually as interested in meeting me as he would be in meeting such a genius as Einstein, Millikan, or Mme. Curie—any great scientific intelligence. He would grant me an audience, simply because he would be anxious to hear what I have to say."

"To say the least, doctor, he is shrewd," Peter murmured.

"Ah, yes! That's what Avery here says.—That's what

my wife says.—Mr. Lu is three hundred years old. More wisdom, more shrewdness, more canniness is compressed into that skull of his than into the skull of any man living today."

"And a diabolical understanding," Professor Van Zant added, in his thin, harsh voice.

"YES, YES!" THE doctor said impatiently. "Yet no matter if Mr. Lu's brain—his fabulous jade brain—contains all the knowledge of all the ages, he must possess—because he is human—some human weakness. Vanity! Why, otherwise, does he let no man look upon the ugly, the horrible scar that is his face?—Vanity! He is a horribly grotesque object, no doubt. Yet he must have his streak of vanity, because no man can live to any age without some streak of vanity. Well, what can he be vain about? Very probably, his brain—and his remarkable age. What do you say, Moore?"

"You are probably quite right. I should call it a very shrewd guess, doctor."

The black eyes looked at Peter almost fondly. "Yes! I am shrewd! First, I must gain access to Mr. Lu. First, I must know how to make my way into that remarkable palace under the Lake of the Flying Dragon.—But wait! I do not expect you to give me that secret yet. Avery, we must ask you now to excuse yourself. You will kindly wait outside until I call you. And if I find you have been eavesdropping, I will have your head lopped off!"

This was said with a certain heavy jocularity, yet Peter was sure that Dr. Strang would not hesitate to have the head of this man—or of any man—lopped off if it would advance the doctor's cause in any way, and provided he had that despotic privilege.

Perfectly submissive, Professor Van Zant let himself out and closed the door.

Pitching his voice very low, Dr. Strang continued, "I will tell you, frankly, Moore; there is only one man in the length and breadth of China whom I feel I can securely trust in this affair. And that man, as you may have guessed, is yourself."

Peter discovered then what he had suspected was Dr. Strang's great fault: carelessness. The doctor had assumed that the man lying on the bunk was either unconscious or asleep. He assumed that whether or not Bill Montgomery was asleep, sooner or later he would get around to killing him. But any assumption of this sort was an act—or a confession—of carelessness. Bill Montgomery might live to tell about all this; he might somehow escape death at the hands of the doctor's hirelings. The doctor, in short, took unnecessary chances; and in a dangerous game such as he was playing, a man cannot take the slightest chance.

"Van Zant," the doctor was saying, "is helpful—the very soul of willingness. But he is weak. At the least hint of torture, if he was captured, he would blab.—This is no game for weaklings. It is a dangerous game for men like you and me—men who are strong and fearless."

One corner of Peter's mind was aware that the man on the bunk was no longer snoring. But he hoped that Bill would not attempt to settle this issue with his fists.

"Moore," Dr. Strang went on, "you are going to be my adviser. You are going to share the rewards.—Listen!" His voice dropped to a whisper; his hypnotic black eyes seemed to glow redly with an inward fire. *I am going to kill Mr. Lu!*

14

THE PLAN

THE DOCTOR STARED at Peter, watching for the effect that that startling announcement would have on the young man.

Peter took it calmly. His gray eyes narrowed a little, it was true; and a flicker played across his mouth muscles. Otherwise he betrayed no agitation or excitement—largely because he had been anticipating the announcement.

Dr. Strang came closer to him, grasped a handful of his flannel shirt at the shoulder, stared intently into his eyes. "You think I'm mad!"

"No," Peter said. "Over-optimistic."

"You think I'm no match for him!"

"That's what I think, yes. He is wonderfully protected. I grant that you might enter that palace, doctor. But you won't get within a hundred feet of Mr. Lu. Don't forget, he is a mechanical wizard. For example: I am an electrical engineer. I know something about electric lighting. But his system of illumination in that place completely baffled me. There were no lights, yet the place was flooded with light. That may mean nothing to you. But to a man like me, to whom lighting is a science, it is as incredible as if Mr. Lu, before your own eyes, brought a dead man back to life."

Dr. Strang was slowly shaking his head. "You don't understand," he said. "My whole point has escaped you. I have no intention of charging in there and killing him with weapons—or my own hands. You should credit me with greater intelligence than that. But I do say that I can fascinate him with the amazing things—all very true— that I can tell him about the human brain. I can keep him interested for weeks—months!

"Little by little, I let him realize—oh! by the subtlest of hints that I will drop and continue to drop—that the functioning of his own brain is not quite what it should be. By this time we will be the closest of friends. I have battered down his resistance to letting his horrible grotesqueness be seen by other eyes. We will be intimates!—You doubt it?"

"Go on," Peter encouraged him.

"Little by little I will urge upon him the necessity of a brain operation. If he consents to an operation, I have merely to plunge my knife into his spinal cord."

"But if he refuses to let you operate?"

Dr. Strang gave an impatient shrug. "We will be intimates by then, anyhow. I will have a dozen—a hundred— opportunities a day to kill him off! Oh, I don't intend to do it too early in the game. He will unquestionably admire me tremendously. I will learn his secrets.—Moore, why are you so incredulous?"

"I still say you're suffering from over-optimism."

"But you don't realize my capacity for winning his admiration, his respect, his friendship! Think how lonely he must be! Think what a relief it will be for him to have at last a friend—one who understands. One who does not shudder at his scar of a face, his deformed body! He will open his heart to me! More important, he will open his brain to me! I will learn his secrets. How he compounds that powerful blue poison, one drop of which, if dropped into a stream, will kill a man who drinks of that stream a mile below! You've heard of that blue poison?"

PETER NODDED. "I'VE seen a man who died of it—the sting of the Blue Scorpion!"

Dr. Strang said excitedly, "Is it true that the body of the victim turns a luminous sapphire blue, that the eyes turn as black as balls of ebony?"

"Yes, doctor. And the brain turns to liquid—a milky, jelly-like liquid of about the consistency of the whites of eggs."

Dr. Strang grunted excitedly. "Ah!" he cried. "But that isn't all I will learn. I want the secret of his immortality. I want the hundreds of secrets which he, of all men on earth, possesses. And when I have them, I shall kill him!" Panting, he added, "Of course I am over-optimistic! Isn't it enough to set any man's brain afire? Think what it means! I shall become the most powerful man in the world! I shall control the world! The secret of that poison and the secret of perpetual life—those two alone—will make me the most powerful man in the world. You know that; you can't deny it. I could kill off the population of entire cities!—I would be the world's dictator!—Shall be! *I shall be Mr. Lu!*"

The madness in Dr. Strang's eyes was now so evident that Peter felt uncomfortable. But he knew that the medical man relished an argument, and so he gave him a good one.

"Doctor," he said, "you've overlooked a very important difficulty."

Dreams of power and glory faded from the red-rimmed eyes. "What is it?"

"You say—and I admit—that Mr. Lu will have heard of you. Certainly, he will know of your fame as a great surgeon. But hasn't it occurred to you that he would also know of the troubles you got into with the authorities in San Bernardino? Wouldn't he know that you had to leave America to escape arrest? Won't this knowledge make him suspicious of you?"

Dr. Strang replied angrily that he could explain the San Bernardino matter to anyone's satisfaction. It was remarkable, Peter reflected, how convincingly criminals are all able to justify crime. They generally blamed others.

"I depend on my nimbleness of wit to answer any question which Mr. Lu may raise—to his complete satisfaction. It was politics which was responsible for what happened at San Bernardino. Certain jealous politicians had it in for me; I was framed."

Peter had almost forgotten that one. Dr. Strang's kind were always framed!

"I CAN EXPLAIN it all to Mr. Lu," the doctor said vigorously. "It is a tremendously interesting story that I will tell him some—ah—evening.—The inside story! But that is neither here nor there, Moore. I am determined to make good. Call me over-optimistic, if you wish. I shall show you! I shall win Lu's confidence. I shall steal all his secrets. Then I shall kill him...."

"That, in brief, is my program. For your aid in the undertaking, you will receive such fabulous payment that it is really ridiculous, at this time, to mention terms. Nothing you can demand is too great. I know you are a romantic

idealist; all real adventurers are. There's a streak of the quix-
otic in you, naturally. Therefore, I am proposing this plan
to you, very frankly, on such grounds. Mr. Lu is a yellow
menace to white civilization, and only with your help can
I rid the world of him.

"Moreover, quite as frankly, I tell you that Miss O'Gilvie
is to remain a hostage until I have successfully begun my
negotiations with Mr. Lu. I regret the necessity of using
such pressure on you; but it is, perhaps, necessary. I put it
more strongly than that; your assistance is imperative to the
success of my undertaking. If you will not help.me—if you
refuse to do what I say—I shall open that girl's head. I shall
cut into her brain, and make her an incurable idiot for life!"

Peter had been anticipating that, too. But he did not
betray any emotion. His eyes remained calm and attentive
and thoughtful.

"I see, doctor," he said. "I see that you're determined to
go through with this mad scheme of yours. Now, suppose
you tell me just what I am to do."

The doctor stared at him, then said, "I am glad you are so
sensible, Moore. I've been betting my money on you. You
are cool, and you are clever. You are, actually, the one man
in the world who can help me. Now, this is how you figure
in my plan. Having been in Mr. Lu's palace, you not only
know your way back—and will be able to lead me—but the
very fact that you were permitted to escape with your life,
the very fact that you have been permitted to live, is proof
that you are somehow in Mr. Lu's good graces. Certainly,
he will not deny you entrance again. Doubtless, there is
something he wants from you. I want you to go there and
find out what it is, promise to carry out his wishes!"

"Or be killed," Peter said.

"Bah! You won't be harmed."

"Or, perhaps," Peter said dryly, "we won't even get in. There's only one way to enter that lake, you know—by a narrow pass guarded by a village."

The doctor said impatiently, "You will send word to him from the village. He will see you.—He will see us both. We will start early tomorrow morning. My guards will take you to a meeting place on the river. You will not be harmed unless you attempt to double cross me in any way. I will leave now. I warn you not to attempt to follow me, to track me. If I find that you have gone against my orders, that very moment I will do to that girl what I threatened."

HE WENT TO the door. Peter said, "Let me sum this up, doctor. Correct me if I'm wrong. I meet you tomorrow morning. You and I go to the Lake of the Flying Dragon— just the two of us, and, of course, a guard. Right?"

"Quite right."

"What happens to Professor Van Zant?"

"He remains with my wife and Miss O'Gilvie until you return."

"Very well. So you and I proceed to the lake. We are, of course, immediately captured and taken before Mr. Lu. We won't get nearer to him than a hundred feet, of course. He sits in the apex of a narrow, triangular room with a dazzling blue light burning behind him. Quite terrifying. You must be prepared for surprises."

"I'm prepared for anything!" the doctor cried enthusiastically.

"When we are taken before him, I account for my presence—or rather, my boldness—by stating my willingness to act upon any orders he wishes to give me. And I leave, presumably, to act on such orders. You remain to court his friendship. If I come out of all this alive, I am to be fabulously rewarded. Is that it?"

"You can name your reward!"

"What assurance can you give me that, in our absence, Miss O'Gilvie will be perfectly safe?"

"Take my word, she will be perfectly safe. Please bear in mind, Moore, that I have left no stone unturned. I have spent a fortune—indeed, the bulk of my personal fortune. I am willing to gamble my last dollar on the success of my plan. I have spent money lavishly. I have hired and armed upwards of three thousand of these hillmen. There's nothing they wouldn't do for me. They're mad about me. I am their king! Those three thousand men will be on guard where my wife and Miss O'Gilvie and Professor Van Zant will take refuge. They could not be safer."

Peter was skeptical. "How many people, doctor, know of your plans?"

"No one knows my complete plans but yourself."

"But you have discussed details with your wife and with Professor Van Zant."

"Unimportant details."

"Has it occurred to you that Mr. Lu may somehow know of your plans?"

"Impossible! I have taken every precaution. You will admit, won't you, that I am thorough?"

Peter said quietly, "Yes. Yes. You're thorough."

Dr. Strang opened the door. "I will meet you in the morning. Once again, I warn you that any attempt you might make at double crossing me will be a grievous mistake. Good-night!"

"Good-night," Peter said.

Standing in the doorway, Peter watched the wide, sloping shoulders of the madman as they mingled with the dirty blue of the native guard. He heard the doctor say, with heavy self-importance, "All right, Avery. It's all settled."

Peter pulled the door shut.

THE MOMENT HE did so, Bill Montgomery sat up and swung his feet to the floor. Through puffed eyelids, which reduced his vision to mere slits, he gasped, "Good God, Moore! Aren't you going to do anything?"

Bolting the door, Peter turned slowly and said: "Not so loud. The doctor, in his excitement, completely forgot that you were here. Take this gun. If he comes back, it means he's remembered. And if he does come back, there's nothing for us to do but shoot it out."

He retrieved Bill's gun from the corner of the room, where he had tossed it, and handed it to him. Picking up his own revolver from the foot of the bunk, he dropped it into the holster at his belt.

The man from Montana stood up and started for the door with the gun in his hand.

Peter said quietly, "The moment you open that door, Bill, we die."

"But what are we going to do?"

"Sit tight."

"But I'm trapped! He'll remember that I'm here. He's sure to come back! I'd rather die shooting my way out than be shot here like a cornered animal!"

"Let's use our heads. How much of my conversation with the doctor did you hear?"

"Every word of it!"

"Then you know that there are at least a dozen armed hill men out there. There are doubtless a hundred others scattered about, to keep my men under control. For the present, I'm counting on the doctor's one great weakness—carelessness. It was careless of him to talk so freely with you lying there. It was careless of him not to have you shot immediately. He doubtless intended to get around to it—but he forgot. We are betting on his carelessness. It's the only thing we can bet on. There's nothing we can do, I assure you."

The cattle prince groaned. He began to pace up and down the small area, softly, mechanically beating a palm with a fist, frowning, muttering. He turned suddenly, almost savagely, on the engineer.

"I'm not thinking of myself," he said. "I know you're not thinking of yourself. It's Susan."

"Yes," Peter said. "But there's nothing we can do. By sitting tight, by doing nothing now, we may be able to help her later."

Bill Montgomery expelled his breath explosively. "That maniac isn't coming back!"

"He's evidently forgotten that you were here. In the morning, after I leave, you may have a chance to do something, although I don't know what it could be. When I leave, this guard will be withdrawn. If I'm not given a chance to talk to any of my men, I'll leave a note for you to my most reliable man."

"Chinese?"

"Yes."

"Damn the Chinese!"

"This man is absolutely dependable. His name's Lee Gow. He knows this country. He'll arm all our men—and help you find Susan. I don't know how you can go about it. Frankly, I'm counting on only one thing: the doctor's carelessness. A cog may slip somewhere in this elaborate scheme of his."

"Do you think he was lying about those three thousand armed hill men?"

Peter shook his head.

Bill Montgomery groaned. "Have you ever been in a jam as tight as this before?"

"Nope."

THE MAN FROM Montana walked toward him. "I want to apologize for barging in here the way I did," he said. "I've had you wrong all along."

"Forget about it, Bill."

"I want to take back every one of those damnably idiotic things I said. I deserved a worse beating than I got."

"I'm sorry," Peter admitted, "that we couldn't have had a chin-chin first."

Bill shot out his hand. "I want to shake your hand!" he said.

He gripped Peter's hand. And Peter sensed that the man from Montana had slipped unconsciously into another rôle. He might have said, in a deep, throbbing voice, "When two strong men from the ends of the earth—" or something as fervently dramatic, as suitable to the occasion. The way his head was held, the way in which he threw his shoulders back, was sufficiently eloquent. "Ringed in by foes," his attitude said, "we may be dead ere dawn comes. But we die fighting!"

He relinquished Peter's hand, and going to the bunk, seated himself on the edge of it, his hands on his knees, his arms bowing out, his attitude one of deep thought. This new attitude said plainly, "Face to face with death, let us not despair! There may be a way. Somehow, God willing, we will save her!"

Peter, understanding all this attitudinizing, did not blame him. And he knew that, however Bill dramatized his big moments, underneath he was fearless, valiant. He liked Bill, and he hoped he could somehow get Bill out of this mess unhurt.

The engineer went to the little window beside the door and looked out. The window faced the east. Squarely in the center of the black panorama, on a distant mountain range, he saw the silvery glow of moonrise. Clotted white clouds in an ink-black sky diffused the white radiance. The rim of the moon appeared and transformed the blackness of the ravine into a splendor of silver and black. The great power house became a giant cube of the precious metal. The river was ebony.

The moon rose above the mountain, white and glittering with hardness, as if its surfaces were of diamond. It made the construction camp a bivouac. The cold, white light glittered on rifles. The camp was full of men with rifles— hundreds of them.

Dr. Strang might be careless of details, but in his larger plans he was extravagantly thorough. At least a thousand of his men were waiting, to make sure that Peter Moore kept that early morning rendezvous.

15

THE JADE LADY

FIFTY HORSEMEN PICKED their way, single-file, through a narrow pass in the mountains just south of the dam. Dr. Luigi Strang and Professor Avery Van Zant were, respectively, the first and second men in the line. The others were armed hillmen. The rising moon silvered their new rifles, sparkled on their new spurs. It had cost Dr. Strang a fortune to hire and caparison his "army." But he did not begrudge a dollar spent. Compared to the vast wealth he soon would control, his total expenditures were as a drop of water is to a mighty ocean.

He was exultant. The nearness of success intoxicated him, and the ease with which he had handled Peter Moore, reputedly so hard-boiled, put new plumes in his vanity.

"We can't fail now," he told his companion enthusiastically. "I compare myself to a mighty wave, sweeping everything before it. I am like Napoleon returning from Elba. I gain power as I advance. There is nothing I can't accomplish, Avery! I have the sense of having the world, here, in the very palm of my hand! I am indomitable!"

Perhaps half an hour's ride from the hydro-electric construction camp, the doctor remembered that he had left Bill Montgomery lying on the bunk in Moore's shack.

He had intended to have him killed. But in his excitement he had neglected that detail.

Yet having recalled his negligence, he did not even rein in his horse. "I will attend to that conceited young ass later," he said. "Remind me, Avery, to have him shot."

Professor Van Zant said nothing. But when his mentor returned to his favorite theme, the irresistible triumph just ahead, the professor sounded a note of caution. He said in so many words that pride had been known to precede historic collapses.

"But nothing can halt me now!" the doctor declared. "I am, to all intents and purposes, already the master of the world! Nothing can stay me! This is a historic occasion, Avery—one of the times you have heard about—the time when a tide rises in a human life which makes one man the master of human destinies. This tide of mine will carry me to an overwhelming triumph!"

THEY CAME, AT the end of an hour's brisk ride, to a hut that occupied the very center of a small plateau. It had once been a shepherd's hut—so many years ago that none of the hillmen with whom the doctor had talked could recall when it was last occupied.

All about the little hut, hillmen were standing or grouped about small fires. The doctor's army! His legion, the loyalty of which he had purchased with such an extravagant outlay of gold!

Lights were burning in the hut, and the door was open. Karen Strang was standing in the doorway, her slim figure silhouetted against the orange glow, her hair faintly gleaming like a golden cap.

She turned and went into the room as her husband and

"I'll cure you of your dislike of me!" cried the mad surgeon.

the other men rode up and dismounted. Dr. Strang told the professor to wait outside. The doctor strode into the hut. He swaggered.

"Wait outside with Avery. I have something to say to Susan," he said to Karen.

Karen's cool, brilliant blue eyes looked at him for a moment, then she said quietly, "Very well, Luigi. Is everything arranged?"

"Yes! Moore is absolutely acquiescent. He will do just what I say. Of course, he had no choice. He acknowledged my mastery of the situation." His wife went out.

He glanced at the pale girl standing in a shadowy corner. But he seemed unaware of her. He clasped his hands behind him and began to walk back and forth across the room, opposite a stack of rifles in a corner to the open door. Presently he paused long enough to shut the door, then he continued his restless pacing.

Susan followed him with expectant, apprehensive eyes. She was quite certain now that Dr. Strang was a madman, and she only wondered what form his eccentricity would take. Certainly, he was suffering from delusions of grandeur. His attitude was that of a conquering monarch. His eyes had a remote, staring quality that frightened her.

She saw that he was terribly excited; and she wondered if this excitement might not make him actually dangerous, if that brilliant, twisted brain might not strike off on almost any tangent.

When he spoke to her he was calm enough. He stopped pacing presently and came toward her, still with his hands clasped behind him. He came very close to her and looked down into her large dark eyes. He nodded his shaggy head several times. In his beard his wet red lips were smiling.

Softly he said, "Susan, you are very beautiful. You are the most beautiful woman in the world. You are so wistful! Your eyes are so soft, so appealing! Underneath your loveliness there is such fire, such valiance. I love you, Susan!"

Helplessly, Susan looked up into his intent black eyes. Her heart was racing. But she tried not to betray her fright. She felt that she must not lower her eyes from his for an instant; that the firmness of her will, directed through her eyes, was holding at bay, as if it were an animal, crouched, ready to spring, the insanity lurking in his eyes.

"I adore you, Susan. You are such a lovely little thing. So slim! So gallant! So charming!—You must know, of course, that that woman outside means nothing to me. She is cold and hard and selfish. I have no use for her; she does not count. She is already, as far as we are concerned, out of the picture. Perhaps I shall kill her. I haven't yet decided; there are so many things on my mind. But I wanted to take this time to reassure you. Don't be worried, my angel. You have nothing to fear. You are under my protection.—You understand me fully?"

SUSAN, WANTING TO scream, said through parched lips, in a thin little whisper, "I understand."

He took a deep breath, swelling out his chest. "You are to be the queen of the world, my angel! Yes—I am to be the king, and you are to be the queen."

There was now no expression in his eyes. Nothing but that terrifying, staring vacancy. Susan dared not utter the whimper of awful despair that was in her throat. White and expressionless, she only looked up.

Dreamily, he repeated, "You are to be the queen—my lovely, gallant little queen!—I will tell you my secret. I am going to kill Mr. Lu and possess myself of his secrets. I may be away for days—weeks—perhaps months. But you will be safe. My queen is to have a bodyguard of three thousand men. While I am away, I shall be thinking of you—adoring you. Susan, you love me, don't you?" |

Susan could not answer. Her hand flew to her mouth, as if to stifle the scream that hovered there.

"You must say you love me, Susan! It is very necessary. I have taken it for granted. Was I wrong in taking it for granted?"

Susan slid her hand down to her heart and kept it there. Dr. Strang's eyes looked blacker. His shaggy head came closer. He stared at her as if he would, by sheer will power, force that answer from her. His heavy, rumbling voice said, "Susan, you must tell me you love me! I must hear you say it!"

"I can't!" the girl cried.

"You mean—you don't love me?"

"No! No! No!"

He stepped backward, with a puzzled air, as if he had not heard aright. "I don't understand, Susan. You must love me. It is necessary."

Susan said to herself, "How can I stand any more of this? I'll have to scream! I'll faint.—But I *mustn't* faint!"

He had gone to a pile of luggage which was stacked against one wall. From it he selected a small blade bag, the kind of bag that physicians often carry.

He turned his head slowly and looked up at Susan. "You will have to be very patient," he said. He had opened the bag and was pawing about in it. "It is very necessary for you to love me, Susan," he said. "All my work is nothing, if I cannot feel that it is for you, that you are hopeful of my success. Life is useless without love. You are my love."

Dr. Strang paused, with his slim, white hands inside the black bag. There were sounds of movement outside. There were sharp cries—others. Then this agitation subsided.

The madman straightened up. In one of his hands was a small phial; in the other was a surgeon's knife.

Susan, now icy with terror, looked from one hand to the other, then at his face. He was smiling faintly as he came toward her.

"Susan, I am going to cure you of that strange antipathy you have toward me. It is necessary.—It will not hurt. I promise not to hurt you. All I will do is sever a very small nerve in the back of your brain. I won't have to cut through the bone. Generally, I cut through the bone, but I am going to spare you that. Lie dowr—face down—on that cot, my dear. I won't hurt you."

Susan screamed, "No!"

He said gently, almost pleadingly, "Must I use force? I would so much rather not use force.—It is for your good, Susan. You know I would not harm you."

SUSAN RACED TO the door, but Dr. Strang had evidently anticipated that. Before she could reach it, he was there. Panting, she tried to push him away. He had dropped the phial into a pocket. The scalpel he held in his teeth.

He seized her wrists in hands which, despite their fineness, might have been manacles. She could not move. Holding both wrists in one hand, he forced her toward the cot. But he did not immediately place her on the cot. He fumbled with his free hand at the back of her neck. Susan struggled, screamed. She could not escape that searching hand. It closed on her neck. She felt a sudden sharp pressure applied at the base of her brain. A white light seemed to burst in her brain.

Half conscious now, limp in his hands, she resisted no longer. She was aware of sensations, but her muscles had no response. She suddenly smelled a pungent liquid; but whether it was ether, chloroform, or alcohol she could not say. It was as if the life was ebbing out of her brain.

She was lying face down on the cot. His hands were pushing away the hair at the nape of her neck. His fingers touched her skull, here and there, lightly, rapidly. Lightly and madly, they seemed to be dancing all over the back of her skull. Incredibly, they reminded Susan of birds, frantically, blindly, trying to escape—fluttering here and there, in terror pecking away at whatever it was that obstructed their escape.

"It will hurt for only a moment, Susan."

A woman's clear, cool voice intruded. "Oh, this has gone quite far enough! Drop that knife, Luigi."

Susan felt the mad, dancing fingers leave her skull. She commanded herself to move, to sit up. It took all the nervous force she possessed to execute this desire. Fighting down that mental fog.

Ordering her crumpled will to stand by her. Compelling her listless muscles to coordinate. With awful tremblings, she did at last accomplish what she wanted; she turned on her side, dropped her feet to the floor, pushed herself to a sitting position.

Karen was standing above them, a German automatic pistol, a Lüger, in one hand.

It had a long barrel, and the muzzle of it was within a foot of the doctor's heart.

"Put that knife down or I will kill you, Luigi! If you raise your voice—if you make any attempt to call for help—I will shoot you. Drop that knife on the floor!"

Her husband dropped the scalpel. His breath, thick and heavy and somehow red with rage, seemed to gurgle out of that great barrel of a body. "How dare you interfere with me?" His dilating eyes roved from her face to the door. "Where is Avery?" he whispered hoarsely.

"Gone."

Susan, looking at her, felt suddenly cold. She shivered. Karen had worn riding clothes when she had last seen her. She now wore a fantastic thing of vivid jade green—a kind of robe. It came high up on her neck and covered all the length of her arms, except the wrists.

It was the brightest, most intense green Susan had ever seen. It had a life of its own, independent of the woman who wore it. It seemed vibrant. This was an intangible quality, an *essence* quite apart from the material or the amazing intense color. It lent Karen Strang an air of barbaric mystery, of absolute unreality. Taken with it, her hair might truly have been of carved gold, her white face a mask of platinum—or metallic porcelain.

The carved green jade quarter-moons hanging from her ear lobes, and the string of carved green jade amulets at her throat, were the ornaments of a mythological goddess. **SUSAN WAS SUDDENLY** much more afraid of her than she had ever been of Dr. Strang. Even the jade lady's eyes were a glittering metal. She was not a woman of flesh and bones and blood, but a creature compounded of rare metals, in which the breath, the beat, the spark of life magically resided. She had become the essence of all things sinister and unknown.

Dr. Strang's dilating eyes had leaped from the empty doorway to his wife's face. They grew more and more brilliant. The doctor's breath was no longer produced in heavy wheezes, but in silent, quick little puffs. His face had gone slack, flaccid. It was suddenly white, and oily. His lips were no longer red, but colorlessly dark—a nameless, leaden blue. His great bulk was trembling. It was as if he had been suddenly devastated by a glimpse of a stark, hideous fatality.

"You are an agent of Mr. Lu!" he whispered.

"Yes."

"You saved this girl from my knife only because you had orders to deliver her to him!"

"Yes."

A lower whisper, as venomous as the hissing of a cobra, "You devil! You horrible woman!—You vulture! You vampire!"

"I warn you, Luigi," the jade lady said, "that I will kill you if you make any attempt to summon help."

Dr. Strang was softly, desperately, beating his temples with his clenched fists, as if he was trying to arouse some masterly thought that would cope with this incomprehensible surprise.

"You and this girl are to come with me," the jade lady said. "Three horses are outside. You are to ride the black. You, Susan, will ride the gray. I ride the white. You will mount your horses and go where I direct you. Susan will lead, and you will follow. I shall ride last. Come."

16

THE CHARCOAL PAGODA

PETER MOORE WAS looking out the window of his shack when that savage and mystifying attack began. The power house stood out white and sharp in the light of the soaring moon. It was like a fortress, except that it lacked the great, forbidding bulk of a fortress.

It was, in another sense, a monument—the kind of monument that explorers build to mark their farthest advance. Certainly, in the engineer's mind, even at this pessimistic moment, it did not stand for death. Long after his death, it would be doing its work. His great regret was that he would not be here tomorrow when it would begin the fulfillment of its destiny. There was something clean and fine about this power house. He was proud of it; proud, too, of the slim wires strung to those rugged steel masts which would carry sixty thousand volts over hundreds of miles of hills and rivers and deserts. To him, all this was the essence of romance, the stuff of fine dreams.

He was suddenly resentful that he would be unable to finish the project. He wanted to build the other plants; wanted to see the chain working as a synchronous unit. Susan would have been proud of that.

Damn Dr. Strang! No man had so successfully spoiled

another man's plans, or ruined his aspirations, than had this black-eyed madman. Peter wondered what would happen to them in Mr. Lu's palace. What, he desolately wondered, would happen to Susan? The mad doctor had, with his fantastic scheme, completely smashed their lives.

Bill Montgomery, standing there beside him, was occupied with his own thoughts. Long ago, he had ceased to dramatize the situation. The emotions engendered by the imminence of inevitable death cannot be dramatized for any great length of time. The stark fact pushed in on him, numbed him.

Peter knew now that Bill was not afraid. It was simply that his brain was unable to cope with an inescapable doom.

Silently, the two men were looking out the window. It was at that moment that the hillsides all about them became alive with swarms of armed men. These hordes might have been bred from the dark pockets of shadow under the bowlders. They sprang into being as the warriors of the fable sprang, full girt, from the ground where dragons' teeth had been sown. They came in surging waves from the East.

They were barefoot, which meant to Peter that they were river men. Doubtless they had come up this tributary from the Yangtze, in sampans. Leaving their boats downstream, they had slipped from shadow to shadow with the stealth and quiet of ghosts.—But all these stealthy, swarming men wore blue capes over their heads, small capes faintly resembling the burnooses which roving desert tribes of the north wear as protection against the blinding sandstorms! **THEY ATTACKED THE** bivouacked forces which Dr. Strang had left to guard Moore and Montgomery with a swiftness, a deadliness that was appalling. It was as if the hillsides had suddenly burst into flame. The rippling red-blue of rifle fire occurred simultaneously, as if it was timed to a split second. From every quarter it sent up an explosive roar as tremendous, as deafening, as the detonation caused by a mountain rent in half by an earthquake.

There was no doubt in Peter Moore's mind that these attacking hordes were Mr. Lu's men. Their concerted deadliness of attack alone meant that. And there was significance in the blue color of their capes.

Peter seized Bill Montgomery by the shoulders, and with a jerk, pulled him down to the floor. Above the rattling explosions, he shouted, "Safer down here! Chances are, though, they have orders not to harm us."

The man beside him on the dirt floor cried, "I'd rather go out there and take my chances!"

"You wouldn't live ten feet."

"But what chance have we, if they're Lu's men?"

"We've had luck so far."

Bill roared an answer, but Peter was unable to distinguish what it was. Dr. Strang's surprised warriors were now springing to arms. The sharp nitric odor of burned smokeless powder began to seep into the shack. The air shook with the volleys of rifle fire. The ground trembled under the pounding feet of running men. A bullet, perhaps a ricochet, screamed through the roof of the shack. Another shattered the window.

It seemed to Peter that the firing was moving away and upward—toward the top of the dam. Feet were running in that direction. Beyond the flimsy wall he heard a man scream in agony. The scream subsided to a gurgling moan.

The firing drew off. Peter's guess was that Dr. Strang's mercenaries were trying to retreat over the dam, and that Lu's warriors were following, ruthlessly slaughtering them.

"Can you hear me now?" Bill Montgomery shouted.

"Yes!"

"I said, if Lu's men have orders not to harm us, what's to prevent us from fighting our way through them?"

"We can try," Peter said. "Come on!"

He got up and opened the door of the shack. Thin vapors hung in the moonlight—all but invisible gases. Dead and dying men were strewn all over the camp. A hundred men in blue capes were rolling these victims to the rim of the low cliff that overhung the river—cleaning up—leaving no traces. That was like Mr. Lu.

"We'll cut back over the hill behind the power house," Peter said. "Ran!"

They ran down, the path toward the power house. One of the blue-hooded men raised a rifle. Suddenly he pushed it down. Bill Montgomery, aiming as he ran, fired at him. The Chinese sprawled and limply rolled over on his back.

Then the hooded men of Mr. Lu came swarming from every side. The two Americans emptied their guns, then used them as clubs. They fought literally back to back. The ring of hooded men about them pressed closer and closer. Peter lifted his revolver and brought it down on a head. The head vanished. But now he could not lift his hand at all. He and Bill Montgomery were packed in so tightly that they could not move.

PETER'S GUESS THAT they would not be harmed proved

to be a correct one. They were not harmed, They were not touched by a single hand. They were simply rendered powerless by the pressure of that deep, silent human circle. The men closed in upon the two Americans more and more tightly, as the iris of an eye closes to diminish the brilliance of light; and presently they were unable to move a hand or a leg, could scarcely breath.

The man from Montana was panting and cursing. What he would do to these yellow devils if he could only move his hands! It was the colorful, sulphurous language of the cowboy at bay—blasphemies which he had learned at roundups, on night herd, when the human spirit is so sorely tried by brute stubbornness and folly.

But he soon lost heart. He gasped, "Pete, what the hell are these coyotes going to do to us?"

"I wish I knew."

The immediate intentions of the "coyotes" was, however, promptly evidenced. Sacks of tough blue cloth were bound down about the Americans' heads; their hands were lashed behind their backs. The cattle prince's profanity, his dire threats, now came muffled, though no less valiant. He was—by this and by that!—going to even matters up! It might take long, because it was an ambitious program, reducing all this yellow humanity to so much pulp! Nevertheless they'd see, some day!

Peter's desires were somewhat less ambitious. All he wanted was to get Bill, Susan and himself out of this deadly situation somehow—to reach the haven of Shanghai or Pekin.

Hands touched them now, but these were the hands of guidance—always there, instantly ready, in case either of the white men stumbled. They were taken up the path to the dam. They were led across the dam. A thin, cold, mountain wind filtered through the cloth bag and carried to Peter the smell of fresh blood. But the firing had ceased. He supposed that Lu's men had finished their mopping up. He wondered if any of Dr. Strang's mercenaries had survived. He doubted it.

Once across the dam, he lost all sense of location. They were being taken down the side of the hill, but as this hill was domelike, it was hard to guess in which direction they were going.

Presently he heard the nervous chatter of horses' hoofs on the stones. Hands lifted him into a saddle and placed his feet into bone stirrups.

He called to Bill, and the man from Montana answered, "Any idea where this outfit's taking us?"

Peter didn't know. The horsemen started. There must have been a hundred of them. They rode along at a brisk trot, slowing only for steep descents, or where the going was exceptionally rough. The wind seemed to be striking Peter mostly on the right side. He knew the prevailing winds in this section of the country were from the north, and so he assumed their course of travel to be westerly. Yet he had no clear idea of the direction, and he presently lost all sense of time.

THAT SWIFT RIDE across the hills might have consumed fifty minutes or several hours. He was too preoccupied with trying to stay in the saddle to think of much else. His horse was sharp-gaited and nervous, but a man rode on either side of Peter for the purpose of keeping him in his saddle. They talked briefly. He gathered that they were late for some appointment, and that they must make better time. He learned that all of Lu's men had withdrawn from the vicinity of the power plant; that half of them were following the horsemen afoot, the other half returning to the sampans a few miles down the river.

The two Chinese who rode, one on either side of him, were evidently the leaders of this expedition. He presumed that he was being taken to wherever Susan was, and that he and she were to be placed under a strong guard. They would—presumably—be taken together to the sampan fleet, which would proceed down the river to the Yangtze, and up the Yangtze to its most westerly navigable point. From there, they would proceed by horseback to the Lake of the Flying Dragon.

This seemed logical enough. But what was to become of Bill Montgomery? Was he to be taken to that fabulous palace, too? Had Dr. Strang and Professor Van Zant also been captured?

Peter was suddenly conscious of a damp chill in the air. It was different from the dry air through which they had been trotting, and he supposed that they were down amongst trees, in some deep ravine.

The cavalcade stopped. Peter was lifted down from his horse. The hood was snatched from his head, and he found himself standing beside Bill Montgomery, in the apex of an angle which was formed by lines of blue-hooded men. It was a human wedge-shaped group of men, with the two Americans facing the open end at the top.

All about them were the aspiring, melancholy forms of cedar trees, the drooping branches of which looked wet and black in the moonlight that filtered through them. Just ahead, rising into the night, was a tall, familiar structure—a pagoda. It was black as India ink, except where the moonlight silvered the projections of its narrow upper stories.

The man from Montana gasped, "What place is this?"

"It's called the Charcoal Pagoda," Peter answered. And added with grim humor, "It's supposed to be haunted by a white dragon forty feet long, that breathes live steam and lights its way with fire-green eyes."

As he concluded that fable, a glow of light appeared in the doorway of the Charcoal Pagoda. In color it was a dazzling, sapphire blue. Coming from a source within the pagoda, it laid a path of sapphire blue light across the ground to the feet of the two Americans. Mist or vapors coiled and swam about in the shaft of dazzling blue; and the chill sweat of fear broke out on Peter's forehead. Only once before had he seen that particular vivid sapphire light. It had blazed at the end of a triangular room, in the cave of the Blue Scorpion!

17

BEFORE THE THRONE

THE TWO LINES of Chinese closed behind Peter Moore and Bill Montgomery. Gently but insistently, they were urged toward the door of the pagoda.

Bill Montgomery said quietly, "Something tells me that we are never going to walk out of that place alive. If we don't—so long!"

A man behind them slashed the bindings at their hands. And Bill said, "My hands are numb. But—shall we try to make a break for it?"

Peter shook his head. "No use. I'll do my best to get you out of this."

"Do you know what it means?"

"I think so. I think we're all keeping an appointment with Mr. Lu."

"Not here!" Bill said.

"We'll soon know."

Their voices were the only sounds, except for the faint sighing of the wind in the melancholy cedars. No sound came from the pagoda. The men all about them were so silent that they seemed not even to be breathing.

The blazing, sapphire light, now shining in their eyes, prevented them from seeing the man lying at the foot of the pagoda steps until they were almost upon him. The man was dead. It was Professor Van Zant, and his throat had been slit. His head lay in a pool of blood, and blood still trickled from the slash.

For the first time, Bill Montgomery's courage seemed to falter. He grasped his companion's arm and whispered, "Is this what's going to happen to us?" The hand on Peter's arm was trembling a little.

"Steady, Bill!"

The cattle prince lifted his head, lifted his chest. The blue light on his face was ghastly. "I'm not afraid!"

"No," Peter said. "You've done nothing to worry about."

Slowly, with elbows touching, the two men walked up the steps. And behind them the lines of men closed in at the foot of the steps. It all reminded Peter, as they approached the doorway of that pagan temple, of a death march; one-two, one-two, one-two. No sound other than the soft thumping of their feet on stone. The sapphire light glaring on their faces made everything grotesque. It gave to everything it touched a stark, macabre quality.

Suddenly it impressed Peter Moore as a scene from some night thousands of years ago. He and this other man were entering a temple of dark and awful mystery—two human sacrifices to some dark and awful god. They had displeased this god, and he was about to visit his wrath upon them.

The sapphire light, filled a large and lofty room with walls of blistered black. There were no windows. At the far end was a latticed door, beyond which was darkness. The sapphire light was an affair of brass shell, suspended from the center of the ceiling by fine brass chains which seemed to be blue incandescent wires. Vapors rose swirling from the heart of the sapphire glare.

BUT PETER NOTICED these details only incidentally, for he had seen Susan, lying in a crumpled heap beneath the brass shell. He heard Bill Montgomery utter a grunt of horror, but paid no heed to him.

Susan was lying on her side, with her head pillowed on her arm. Fearfully, he touched her face, her neck. She was warm. At his touch, she stirred. Her eyes partially opened and stared at him dazedly. They opened wider.

She cried, "Peter!—Oh, darling!" And struggled up. She folded both arms fiercely about his neck, then held him off and stared at his face. When he had lifted her to her feet, she gasped, "You look so dreadful in this light!"

So did Susan, for that matter; she looked ghastly. But she was unharmed. She was suddenly aware of Bill Montgomery, although he was no longer aware of her. His profile was presented to her, and he was staring with open mouth, as if his breathing had been suspended.

Peter followed the direction of Bill's gaze, and was suddenly spellbound.

Clinging to him, Susan whispered, "It's Karen Strang!"

Against that wall, on a pagan altar of carved ebony, sat the jade lady. Like a priestess of some ancient, mystic cult, she sat with chin erect, with hands crossed in her lap. From a brazier on either side of her, white smoke mounted to the ceiling in thin quills. On either side of the bench stood an ebony post, perhaps four feet in height. Similar posts were fixed in the floor at the foot of the steps. From each of the posts beside the bench to each of the posts at the foot of the steps ran a heavy bronze chain. The individual links must have been two inches in diameter., But there was no chain between the posts at the bottom of the steps, to guard the jade lady against approach.

Peter did not know that her gown was of vivid green, because its color seemed to come from the sapphire light above. But even in the blue light her hair was metallically golden and her face was like porcelain. He sensed, as he stared at her, the same thing that Susan had sensed; this woman was hardly human, but rather a creation of metals or ceramics, magically invested with the breath and throb of life.

She was a sinister idol, at whose feet a thousand barbarians might devoutly have knelt. She was a goddess of all the black arts. She was an incarnation of the mystery of all that mortal man would never know. Though a white woman, she was a symbol of all that was cryptic in the deathless lore of Asia.

Yet Peter Moore, sensing all this, tried to deny the feeling that all of this was—must be—occurring on a night thousands of years ago. He logically informed himself that she, like the blue light and like the black pagoda, was but one more manifestation of Mr. Lu's incredible whimsicality.

A FAINT, EERY sighing from the darkened room beyond the latticed door distracted Peter momentarily from the jade priestess, but his quick glance discovered nothing.

Trying to order his senses, trying to compel himself to accept this weird scene calmly, he became aware that the glittering eyes of the jade lady were focused on Bill Montgomery.

He glanced at Bill. The man from Montana still stared,

as if he was actually under hypnosis. His jaw was ajar; his breathing was seemingly suspended. He could see only the woman enthroned on the carved ebony altar.

The lips of the jade lady moved. The faintest of whispers—hardly more, than the rustling ghost of a sound—came from her.

"Here."

That was all. Only the single, simple imperative. And it was addressed, singularly, to the cattle prince. She touched the bench beside her.

This, Peter told himself, was absolutely incredible. Why did that shocking creature wish Bill Montgomery to sit beside her? She was certainly an agent, a tool, perhaps a slave of Mr. Lu's. Call her what one would, she was obedient to the schemes of the Blue Scorpion. Was that why she wished Bill Montgomery to sit beside her?—To witness what?

Chilling possibilities occurred to Peter Moore in answer to the last question. Was it the destruction, in some horribly ingenious Oriental way, of himself and Susan?

He remembered something that had previously seemed of slight importance. That metallic creature, Susan had once mentioned, was in love with Bill Montgomery. Therefore—Oh—preposterous! Peter said grimly to himself, "Not mixing love with work—not that woman!"

She had married Dr. Strang at Mr. Lu's bidding, so that she could make infinitely thorough reports on the mad project of that brilliant, twisted intellect. And in this, again, Peter saw the workings of a mind too Oriental, too devious for him to comprehend. And Peter understood the Oriental mind rather well, too.

If Dr. Strang had seemed to threaten the Blue Scorpion's supremacy, why had the powerful Mr. Lu not simply had him shot or stabbed? The Jade Brain could sometimes work with the stabbing directness of a lightning bolt, and it could also be as circuitous as the beclouded attack of an octopus. What had—or would be—the doctor's fate?

Peter asked Susan what had become of Dr. Strang. She did not know. He had vanished. Susan hardly heard him, for she was engrossed by the jade lady.

Bill Montgomery was walking slowly forward, like a man gripped by some absorbing preoccupation, toward the waiting woman. He gave a little shrug, as if to say, "Well, who cares? What does it matter?"

He proceeded to the ebony altar and slowly mounted the six broad steps which led to the little platform on which the bench was placed. He turned about and seated himself beside Karen. Her head slowly turned, the blue light glinting in her golden cap of hair. She studied his puffed, bruised face for perhaps half a minute.

Folding his arms on his chest, sitting as erectly as if he were a king, the cattle prince ignored her. There was a faint grin upon his swollen lips. It occurred to Peter that that lion-hearted young man might very possibly be enjoying himself, as if he had automatically slipped into a rôle in what he had decided must be *opéra bouffe*—whimsical Oriental farce, laid in a pagoda that was a relic of a forgotten Chinese epoch, staged by what was perhaps the most imaginative, most sinister figure that China had ever produced! Or was he merely prepared with that plucky grin on his swollen lips to meet whatever fate had in store for him?

Certainly, preparations for whatever was about to happen must now be complete.

Susan, with one arm tightly about Peter's waist, was shivering, making little whimpering sounds.

"I did all this," she said. "If I hadn't let Dr. Strang bully me into betraying you, this would not have happened."

As Peter started to reassure her, a voice anticipated him.

"Yes," it said. "You did all this!"

A soft, thin, whispering voice it was, so cold that it sent fresh shudders through Susan.

Peter had spun half about, to face the latticed door. He knew now, quite definitely, that their host was present; that the man whom all Asia called the Blue Scorpion was in that darkened anteroom!

18

THREATS

SUSAN WAILED, "DON'T go in there!" For the suddenly rigid body of the man beside her had seemed to her to indicate his intention of plunging through that latticed door.

But Peter needed no restraint. He had altogether too much respect for the Oriental genius in the next room to commit such foolhardiness. He was tense, however. Doubtless Mr. Lu had reasons for preferring to conduct this audience with himself seated in darkness. It was mandatory that no man should look upon the hideous mass of scar tissue that was Mr. Lu's face; no human eye should see that horribly malformed body of this Oriental monster with the fabulous brain of jade.

The wintry whisper said, "I presume that you remember, Mr. Moore, what our bargain was?"

Peter, thinking of the heads of the three red-haired men, nailed up in the sapphire blue box, shuddered. He knew what was in store for him and for Susan. He only hoped that their death would be swift and merciful. If that beast made Susan suffer—

Yet why should he hope for such charity from the hands of this monster? Characteristically, Mr. Lu would submit them to some unique form of torture which would give him pleasure.

The soft, chilling whisper said, "Then, you do remember?"

"I remember," Peter said heavily.

"Yes-s-s. In return for your silence, I gave you your life. I relied on you to impress upon Miss O'Gilvie the seriousness of that bargain. She has broken that silence, violated our agreement, betrayed my trust. And the penalty is death for both of you. Death!"

Susan's arm was about Peter's waist and was jerking convulsively. She was leaning heavily against him. He could feel the rapid rise and fall of her breast against his side as she breathed.

"Steady!" he whispered.

The icy, soft voice went on, "You know, Mr. Moore, that those who know more than I deem safe—die." An indistinguishable murmuring sound came from the darkened room. Then, "Let us leave this subject for a moment—dangling, as it were, like a keen, two-edged sword. Do not forget, as I go on, that it dangles there, prepared at any instant to drop, and, dropping, to strike both of you dead!"

Impetuously, Susan threw back her head and looked up, as though some gleaming blade did hang, dangling, there, suspended above Peter and herself by some magic thread. She was shivering uncontrollably, and her teeth were audibly chattering.

The whisper, like a breath from the shadow under a glacier, went on. There was a sense of marching, of irresistible onwardness, about the power behind that quiet voice. One sensed a crushing, inescapable force, as if Mr.

Lu was not a man in grotesque form, but a gigantic cold machine that nothing on earth could escape, once the monster mechanical mind had been fixed upon it.

"**I HAVE A** certain use for you, Mr. Moore. I have been interested in you for a number of years. You are a genius in the field of the radio. You are almost a genius with other forms of electricity. By that I mean, you do the best you can with the sorry paraphernalia at your command. I have amused myself by having your recent activities very closely observed. I have placed small distractions in your way. I have occasioned you trivial annoyances, because I was curious to test your ingenuity. And I have merely confirmed my fixed opinion of you: you are almost a genius."

The soft, chilling whisper paused. Peter, staring at the latticed door, tried to form in his mind a picture of what the speaker looked like. Were there eyes in that hideous scar which was Mr. Lu's face? Or was he blind?

"The trouble, Mr. Moore, is that the materials which are placed at your disposal are as crude, actually as useless, as the wooden toys of a river coolie's child. It amazes and amuses me to hear of your herculean labors.—Ah! If those massive machines were only worthy of you! Let me repeat, you are a genius at electricity, as the world knows electricity; but what a poor thing it is! With thousands of sweating coolies at your beck and call, you cast a great concrete dam, while thousands of other sweating coolies bring to your construction camp the ponderous machines which will be set spinning by the rush of water from this dam.— What waste! What abysmal ignorance! At the top of your penstock is a water gate of steel weighing eighty tons. The rotating element of one of your electro-turbines weighs

As the hole appeared in the floor, Susan screamed.

one hundred and seventy-five tons. Am I right? Correct me if I am wrong."

Puzzled, Peter said quietly, "You are right, Mr. Lu."

"What colossal waste! Tons, tons, tons of steel, brass, copper and insulating materials! Thousands upon thousands of tons of concrete! It dismays me! It infuriates me!—That you with your genius should waste your time guiding into place these tens and hundreds of thousands of tons of useless materials! Merely to send forty-eight thousand kilowatts at sixty thousand volts, down copper wires! Would you use a cannon to kill a housefly? Would you employ a thousand elephants to uproot a sapling?—Ah! You do not understand. You are perplexed. You are an engineer, and you want facts, not poetry.—I shall give you facts!"

Mr. Lu's faint, icy whisper paused again. From behind that lattice he was no doubt studying Peter Moore, weighing him, considering him. And Peter, enthralled by the power behind that wintry whisper, wondered why Mr. Lu was so fond of the color blue. His symbol was the blue chalk pyramid; blue was his favored light. Could it be, Peter asked himself, that Mr. Lu could see by no other light, that his optic nerve was sensitive to no other color?

The whisper continued, "You spend months of time, thousands of dollars, to build a great, cumbersome machine to transform water power into electric current. Yet I have a device which will produce more power than your completed chain of power plants—and I can hold it easily in my two hands! I have known the secrets of electricity for more than two hundred years. I was generating electric current—*in unlimited volume,* and at any voltage or frequency desired—before your Edisons, your Watts, your Faradays, your Ampères, your Teslas were born!

"STEINMETZ, WITH HIS simple mathematical equation and the picturesque graphs he derived from it, came nearer my secret than any man who has ever lived, yet he was a thousand epochs away from the discovery. I, too, worked from the simplest of mathematical formulas. But where all those others—your historic great ones—stumbled or fell, or were tempted down easy paths, I went on and found the truth and made it mine!

"Electricity, electrical power, is my slave. I do not cater to it with great masses of concrete and steel and copper and brass and rubber. I harness energy that is at our fingertips—the cosmic flux. I tap the inexhaustible reservoir of power latent in every square inch of air or soil or wood or steel! Do I desecrate the beauties of nature with hideous masses of concrete, with monstrous structures, with offensive steel pipes which coil like pythons? Oh, no!

"Do you wish more electric power than is generated by all the monster hydro-electric plants at Niagara Falls? Very well! I place in certain juxta-position two elements. That is all."

The cold, soft whisper stopped again. Peter, dimly perceiving Mr. Lu's object in talking thus, waited. He presumed that the Blue Scorpion was telling the truth, and that he was not exaggerating. Still in the shadow of an incalculable doom, the engineer was conscious of another, almost equal excitement. If he could only possess this amazing secret!

"You are wondering," that chill whisper went on, "why I am taking the pains to tell you all this, Mr. Moore. Permit me to tell you that it has never been my wish that you and I should be enemies. I have always known that you could serve me well. You have an original and scientific mind. You are ingenious. You have patience. With the proper materials at your disposal, with a thorough understanding and knowledge of my own discoveries and experiments, you could go on to scientific triumphs which would dwarf any contribution that any man has ever made to scientific knowledge.

"I could, if I saw fit, place at your disposal unlimited sums of money and unlimited sources of materials. No scientific investigator in the world's history has had the benefit of such advantages as you would have.

"Permit me to be more explicit. I have invented a machine by means of which miracles may be worked by remote control. You men who deal with your cumbersome balky electrical machines have familiarized yourselves with that phrase. But your meaning of remote control is as clumsy, as crude, as futile as the ponderous, impractical machines to which you apply that phrase. Switches, dials, levers on a switchboard connected by power cables to clumsy machinery a hundred—a thousand—feet away. You call that remote, control! You are trifling with the meanings of words.

"Is the meaning of the word 'remote' a hundred, a thousand feet? Does it imply the use of rubber—and of lead-sheathed copper cables? Not to me, Mr. Moore! To me, the word 'remote' means *far* away—very far away—and conveys the quality of mysterious concealment.

"That is what I mean by remote control. With my machine, when it is perfected, I shall be able to destroy a range of mountains ten thousand miles away! I shall be able to wipe whole cities from the map!—Ah! You are saying, 'The wireless transmission of power!' But in order to understand the principles of my secret you must begin at the very beginning. You must discard all preconceived notions, all textbook ideas of energy and power. There is a greater difference between your conception of power and mine than exists between, let us say, a dying elephant and an ounce of pure radium!

"Is that figure grotesque? It is really not grotesque enough. No comparison is grotesque enough. But it will serve admirably. Your methods are like the dying elephant. Mine are like the ounce of purest radium!

"I HAVE THE mathematical formula, reduced to the simplest and most lucid phrasing, which demonstrates that my idea is practicable.

"But I need fresh enthusiasm—the stimulus, the curiosity, of another brain. I am within an inch of success. I am convinced that once you have grasped the essentials and familiarized yourself with the problem, your brain will supply the answer.

"My proposition to you is that you are to come to my laboratories, in my palace under the Lake of the Flying Dragon. You will live and work there under my protection. You will have absolutely no interference. Your word in your department will be law. You may come and go as you wish. No desire that you may have will be questioned or denied. You will have every comfort, every luxury, every convenience.—Books, materials, tools, scientific instruments—everything that you ask for will be unquestioningly supplied. You have only to give me your word. Your life, and Miss O'Gilvie's, will be spared.—But wait!"

The wintry whisper fell silent again. Susan's arm, about Peter's waist, had relaxed. He could hear her breathing, soft and regular. He knew without asking her, without glancing at her eyes, what her attitude was, what her opinion was. She saw in Mr. Lu's proposal an opportunity for magnificent adventure. She saw herself fitting somehow into this remarkable program. He knew that she would say, if he asked her, that she thought it was perfectly fascinating.

Mr. Lu spoke again. "You have doubtless gathered, Mr. Moore, that I never deal in aimless projects. There is, therefore, no reason for you to suppose that I wish to have this device perfected merely for my own whimsical amusement. I have an ambition. It is to own all the wealth of America. By America, I mean the United States of America. I have not the slightest thirst for power, as such. What I wish, for the present, is wealth. I wish—and intend—to add to my wealth the wealth of the richest nation on earth.

"I intend, Mr. Moore, to acquire the ownership of the United States of America; first of all, by striking at that nation's heart, New York City. The first use for my scientific device, when it is perfected, is to be the complete, utter annihilation of that city. Even now, I have my agents in New York who are only awaiting word from me. Into the hands of each of them will go this device of mine, though in a modified form. You are to be at the controls of the master device. What I mean, Mr. Moore, is that you—if you accept my offer—are to be in complete charge of this phase of my operations.

"PERHAPS YOU REBEL at the thought of this attack on your native land. Let me say this: my plans are so much greater than any merely national purpose, that you would very soon see the wisdom of discarding such a hollow, fatuous word as 'patriotism.' Need I even mention that this is a competitive civilization? As one of the members of my organization, you would be on the right side of the new competition—a fight between me and the civilized world, *in which the world cannot possibly win!* In making your decision, weigh all this carefully.

"You will say that I give you no choice, that I have you in checkmate. That is, unfortunately for you and Miss O'Gilvie, the true situation. You have absolutely no choice. If you prefer death for yourself and for Miss O'Gilvie, you will decline my offer. If you prefer to live, you will enjoy, I can assure you, the fruits of a vast, novel and amazing experience.

"You know that I am a man of my word. You know that I do not beat about the bush. You know that I quickly punish those who offend me. You have seen that my organization is everywhere. You can make no move without my immediate knowledge. My system of espionage penetrates to every corner of the world. My system of protection is absolutely invulnerable....

"Permit me to say one thing more. To decline my offer means not only death for you and this girl; it means a peculiarly dreadful form of death. It means suffering that neither of you can possibly imagine. I have means for torturing your bodies and your brains—your very souls. I can submit you to agonies that will make you beg for death.—Yes! And make you beg for the chance to reverse your decision. So, actually, you have no choice. Yet I will permit you now to say whatever you wish."

Mr. Lu had no need, as far as Peter was concerned, of making such blood-chilling threats. Peter had anticipated them, and there was not the slightest doubt in his mind that Mr. Lu would carry them out. As for the projected attack on America, that might be a colossal lie to test Peter's surrender to the utmost; but Peter, knowing Mr. Lu, feared it was only too real.

Helpless rage possessed Peter. He would rather see himself dead, rather contemplate the prospect of torture, than give his consent to this monstrous proposal. He would rather die any dreadful death than let himself become a party to such an infamous scheme. Yet he would say yes. Obviously, he must say yes, in order to gain time. His consent would automatically free Susan and Bill Montgomery. He would go to the Lake of the Flying Dragon and acquaint himself with Mr. Lu's incredible scientific secrets. And he would somehow contrive to turn these secrets against Mr. Lu.

Peter sensed rather than thought this out. He was too furious for clear thinking. Instinct made him control himself. He must keep his head. He must appear to be deliberate and sincere. But an incident occurred now that shattered these excellent resolutions.

The soft, chill whisper came again, "Karen, that young man has heard too much."

Peter, instantly sensing the grim meaning of that statement, swiftly turned. His eyes photographed that amazing scene: the man from Montana, sitting there with his arms on his chest, his head erect, a thin, proud smile still at his puffed lips; and the jade lady, with her metal hair, her composure like that of a porcelain goddess, seated there on the bench beside him. White quills of incense smoke climbed into the blue-stained air on either side of them.

Before Peter could move, she had acted. A thin blade with a jade handle was clenched in her hand. She lifted it and drove it down, just above Bill Montgomery's hand, into his heart!

19

THE TRAP IS SPRUNG

IT WAS POSSIBLE that Mr. Lu, with his uncanny knowledge of humanity, had devised that as a test, knowing that it would bring Peter Moore's true feelings to the surface. Or it may have been simply that the Blue Scorpion considered Bill Montgomery a dangerous repository for so much information. Whatever his motive may have been, he had ordered Bill Montgomery's death as casually as he might have ordered a servant to fetch him his shoes.

Peter, staring incredulously, watched the dying man start up from the ebony bench with both hands lightly touching the jade handle of the dagger. His amazing vitality, even with death upon him, was protesting against this sudden, unwarned cessation of life.

He toppled forward and fell. His body slid on its side down the ebony steps, and slid on down to the floor, where it slowly, loosely rolled over on its back, with the arms limply outstretched, its open eyes glittering bluely in the sapphire radiance.

For a moment, the shock of it left Peter Moore numb. He did not see the jade lady rising slowly, like an automaton, from the ebony bench. Nor was he aware that Susan had screamed, was screaming once again.

The shock of what he had witnessed seemed to have stunned every nerve in his brain, dulled every sense but that of stark horror. Then, bursting in upon this numbness, came fury—murderous fury. With his bare hands he would kill that monster behind the concealing lattice. He ran to the door. Without thought of consequences, he kicked it open and plunged in. As if the blue light had followed on his heels, the small room in which he found himself began to glow bluely. He took that room in with a swift, sweeping glance.

Except for a figure lying on the floor, the place was empty! An aperture, high in the end wall admitted a single thin beam of moonlight; and this cool white beam fell upon the curiously blue face of Dr. Luigi Strang! His eyes were open and staring. The entire eyeballs were opaquely black—the dull, dense black of ebony. The big, barrel-chested body arched and writhed. Waves of blue seemed to radiate from the doctor's luminous face. The eyes were like lumps of coal on blue satin. Luminous blue hands clawed at the shaggy brown beard, and a bubble of sound came from a mouth that was a blue slit in the midst of the thick brown hair of the beard.

Peter choked back a sob of sheer horror. Sweat broke out clammily on the palms of his trembling hands. He moved shakily toward the dying man.

The Sting of the Blue Scorpion!

THE DOCTOR'S HAIRY, bear-like body, now so hideously, luminously blue, raised itself from the floor in a last tremendous, agonized effort; fell back with a thud. A horrible contortion twisted the bearded face. A thin sigh, like the echo of a tortured cry in hell, was the last sound made on earth by the mad doctor.

Peter, his skin crawling, felt for a heart-beat. There was none. Fury returned to him. Even a creature like Dr. Strang did not deserve a hideous death like this! He straightened up and looked about him for the place of the Blue Scorpion's concealment. He heard two things; the sudden, sharp crackling of rifle fire, and the renewal of Mr. Lu's wintry whisper:

"You are wasting your energies. I am a thousand miles away!"

But Peter could not grasp that. He could not comprehend that Mr. Lu had perfected his own system of radio communication and television so that he could not only converse with Peter as if he were in the same building with him, but could perceive his every movement.

A small door at one end of the room invited scrutiny. Peter ran to it, kicked it open. He found himself in a narrow, black corridor. A door at the end was open. For just a moment a faintly moonlit area of ground beyond served to silhouette a scuttling, crab-like figure. But that could not be Mr. Lu.

Like the deceiving sound of a rattlesnake's warning, which seems to come from all quarters, the chill whisper of Mr. Lu came again. It came from above, from the sides—it came from everywhere and nowhere.

"You are simply wasting effort, Mr. Moore!"

Peter was convinced that the effect was obtained by means of some system of microphonic repeaters. Yet he could never be quite sure. And he could never be quite sure that that scuttling figure he had seen leave the corridor had not somehow constituted Mr. Lu's vision, his eyesight in this place, as well as his hand to strike down Dr. Strang. That scuttling, crab-like figure momentarily reappeared, hastening across the area of moonlit ground. He had paused a moment. When he went on, Peter discerned that he had paused to put on wooden sandals. The sound of them on the rocks came clearly.—*Clip-clop! Clip-clop!*

Peter recalled Susan's description of the Chinese who had followed her in Shanghai, who had been in charge of the gang that had kidnaped her near the landing stages. A spidery man who wore wooden sandals. Certainly, that man was not Mr. Lu.

But Peter did not loiter to speculate upon this, and he made no attempt to follow the spidery figure of the man in the sandals.

The roar of rifle fire suddenly began again, this time close and loud. There was evidently a pitched battle taking place at the very steps of the pagoda. He ran back to the large room. Susan was standing where he had left her, holding both hands to her face, staring at the lifeless face of Bill Montgomery.

The jade goddess was no longer on the ebony altar. She was on her knees beside the man she had killed. She was slowly running distended fingers through her hair, destroying its suave, metallic perfection. She seemed utterly unable to comprehend what she had done under the spell of her master's command. She was softly weeping. Tears dripped out of her eyes—tears shot with the intense blue light of the room, so that they resembled sapphires.

Her hands fell away from her golden hair, and softly,

tenderly, she touched the dead face of the man she had loved.

A BULLET, SLANTING through the doorway, smashed into one of the incense pots at the altar. The pot disintegrated in a small geyser of red embers and white smoke. A powder-puff cloud of smoke rose to the ceiling. Another bullet screamed close to Peter's head and went thumping through a wall.

He said sharply to Susan, "We've got one chance in a thousand to get out of this."

The words were hardly uttered when the two ponderous doors which gave upon the pagoda steps mysteriously, magically, and with incredible swiftness, swung shut. It was impossible to perceive how this had been accomplished by any human agency. Massive steel bolts—they must have been at least four inches square—shot into steel sockets.

Peter ran to the doors and tried to move the bolts. Under his hand they vibrated faintly. Above the sharp crackling of the rifles, he could hear them faintly hum. The bolts would not move. They seemed to be jammed in their sockets. Employing every ounce of his strength, he could not move them. Undoubtedly, they had been activated and were held in place now by electro-magnetic solenoids. The wires controlling the magnets were no doubt cunningly hidden, buried behind layers of metal, so that without heavy tools it would be impossible for him to reach the wires and cut them.

"Come on," he said to Susan. "The back way!"

Taking her by the hand, he led her through the small room where Dr. Strang lay. Susan screamed as she glimpsed the twisted, blue-faced body in the shaft of white moonlight. After the intensity of the sapphire glare, the moonlight looked golden, almost orange.

Holding her hand tightly, Peter pulled her down the corridor. They were within a dozen feet of the door at the end of the passage when, with the same magical, mysterious swiftness, that door also thudded shut. And very faintly, above the rifle fire in front, he heard the same humming of powerful solenoids.

There was now, Peter was certain, no way of escape from the Charcoal Pagoda. Mr. Lu had them trapped. And although Peter had anticipated this, the realization of it was shocking. He wondered, as he half carried Susan back into the large room, why Mr. Lu had stopped talking to him. And he was now certain that the spidery man he had seen scuttling down the corridor had played some important part in Mr. Lu's amazing radio demonstration. Probably this same man was at the controls of the electrical devices which had so magically closed and bolted the pagoda doors.

As they reëntered the large room, Susan screamed again. Then she gasped, "Peter!—Karen's gone!"

Bill Montgomery still lay there, his eyes already glassy with death, but the jade goddess was nowhere to be seen. The sapphire light was growing dim. Either it was burning out, or the mys-terious source of its power was being withdrawn, cut off.

Peter wanted desperately to know where Karen had gone. How had she escaped? Doubtless there were trap doors, secret passages. The pagoda was probably honeycombed with them. Presumably, Karen had escaped by way of some such labyrinth. Peter realized that he might spend a lifetime trying to find—never finding—these secret passages.

As he hesitated, a square hole suddenly materialized in the floor, not twelve inches from where Susan was standing. The hole was six feet square.

Susan screamed. Peter seized her arm and pulled her away from the yawning opening. He led her back to the corridor and fumbled along its walls until he found a door. It gave upon stairs. Peter struck a match. The stairs led up and up, into engulfing blackness. There was at least a half-inch of dust on the steps, and this thick dust was unmarked, proving conclusively that these stairs had not been used in years, perhaps in centuries.

20

THROUGH FIRE

HUSBANDING HIS SUPPLY of matches, Peter led the way. There were smooth black walls, but there were no windows or doors until they had climbed what Peter estimated to be about eighty feet. There he found a door. It opened upon a narrow balcony, hardly more than a ledge. It was too high above the ground, too far from the nearest tree, to risk jumping.

Below them, in the white and black patches of moonlight and shadow, rifles blazed and shouting men surged to and fro. The fight, Peter saw, was still concentrated about the steps of the temple. Evidently, Mr. Lu's men had been instructed to defend those steps, the entrance, at all costs.

Peter and Susan returned downstairs. The sapphire light was burning so dimly now that he could hardly distinguish Susan's features.

Peter said there was only one chance:—"To burn our way out. It's a long chance, but we'll have to take it. We may be smothered. We may be burned to death."

"I'd rather," Susan said, "be burned alive—" and left the thought unfinished.

With his fingernails Peter attacked the black wall beside the altar. He had no weapons, not even a pocket knife. But centuries had softened the cedar. It came off the planks in shreds, though the wood was not rotten. He tried kicking it here and there. He could peel it off, but he could not kick through it. When he had assembled a pile of this shredded wood against the wall, he set it afire. The kindling quickly began to blaze.

Flames attacked the wall, licked up it. Peter stripped off his shirt and fanned the fire, trying to drive the flames against and into the planking of the wall. Flames licked up the wall.

Soon the large room became hazy. The haze became so thick that the dying blue light was invisible.

Susan began to cough. Peter's eyes smarted, and his throat burned. But the flames were roaring now. Gasping, choking, the man and the girl waited for the fire to do its work. Clearly, it was to be a race between the fire and their endurance to withstand the stifling fumes. The dense smoke, each moment seeming to grow denser, might make them unconscious before the fire had done its work.

Peter, risking burns, kicked at the wall where it had been burning longest. He kicked again and again. It gave finally. His foot went through, and he quickly withdrew it. The hole he had made was no larger than four inches in diameter, but it provided a draft. Flames roared through it.

He continued to kick at the planking in the vicinity of the hole, and was thankful that his boots were so stout and that they resisted the flames.

Fire was gushing out of the enlarged hole now, carrying flaming splinters and embers with it. It was larger than a man's head. It grew. Burning splinters fell. In the dense smoke Susan began to cough. It seemed impossible for her to stop. Peter's own throat seemed to be afire. His senses were reeling. Tears caused by the irritating thick, hot smoke were streaming from his eyes. But he continued to kick at the hole.

And suddenly it was large enough.

He told Susan to run, squat down and jump out. "Don't hesitate!" he cried.

SUSAN RAN. SHE stopped, threw her arm over her face, and jumped.

A moment later she cried, "I'm all right. Come on, Peter!"

He followed her. The cold, fresh air of outdoors was like a splash of icy water in his face. He inhaled deep lungfuls and looked about him.

A new note was added to the shouts of the fighting men. They had seen the fire. Bullets thudded into the wall beside the man and the girl. He pulled her to the ground, into the shadow.

Susan, exhilarated by their escape from that flaming-tomb, said excitedly, "Look over there!—Horses! Can't we run for it? Isn't it better than waiting?"

Then she saw what Peter had seen. From the steps and all about the pagoda, wires were strung on posts, driven into the ground. The wires were greenly glowing. They were charged, Peter knew, with high tension current. To touch one of those wires would mean instant electrocution. They were trapped again; and not more than a hundred feet beyond the wires was the grove in which the horses—a half dozen of them—were tethered.

Susan whimpered, "If we could only reach that thicket!"

Hesitating, trying to reason out some method of outwitting Mr. Lu, Peter saw a man near the steps start to run.

He was running toward the wire barricade. When he was within two feet of the wires, pale green flames seemed to shoot out in all directions from his body. The man staggered back with a gurgling scream and collapsed.

Peter said, "Get down! Wait!"

"Where are you going?" she wailed.

"I'll be back in a moment."

Another question melted into a scream of terror as Peter stepped back, ran and leaped back into the hole he had burned through the wall.

Inside, he was holding his breath, making his way through scorching smoke toward the ebony altar. What he wanted was those bronze chains he had seen when he first entered the room.

A chunk of blazing wood fell on his shoulder. Sparks, scattering, burned his face and neck. He found the first chain and tore it free of the posts. His lungs seemed to be bursting, but he dared not inhale this fiery air. He found the other chain and jerked that, too. It did not yield. Outside, he heard Susan scream. He jerked at the second chain again, and it came free. Dragging both chains behind him, he plunged back through the opening and into the fragrant coolness of the out-of-doors.

He dragged both chains to within six feet of the charged wires. One of them he dropped on the ground. The other he gathered into rough loops. He stepped back, then threw the chain, being careful to release his hold upon it. It left his hands like a striking snake. One end wrapped itself about the topmost wire; the rest of it, dangling down, sent bights looping about the other wires. White and green and red flames seemed to gush out of all the wires, crackling and roaring.

He threw the second chain. The flames subsided. In the distance there was a snarling sound, as of some geared machine laboring against a tremendous overload. It was, indeed, laboring against the short-circuit.

PETER GRABBED SUSAN by the hand and pulled her through the wires. They were hot—almost white hot because of the short-circuit—but they were at least for the time being electrically dead.

A bullet shrieked over their heads, with a sound like that of suddenly ripped canvas. Another plowed into the ground at their feet. Peter felt a third rake through the hair at the back of his head.

The man and the girl almost stumbled over the body of a man. There was a small black hole in his forehead, just above his right eye. Peter snatched the automatic pistol out of the dead man's holster. They ran on.

Some one came plunging out of the thicket where the horses were. There was a rifle in his hands. Susan screamed. Peter fired at him twice. The man stumbled, fell to his face, and rolled in the grass.

Peter and Susan ran on into the thicket, mounted the horses that were handiest.

"Up the hill!" Peter said. And he knew that they were leaving this valley of death with very little time to spare. Dr. Strang's men would, no doubt, disband, now that their leader was dead; but until they did so it was perilous to be in this vicinity.

At the top of the hill they reined in their horses and looked down. The Charcoal Pagoda was sending a column of dense black smoke, shot with fiery red, straight into the starry sky. These flames clearly illuminated the scene of battle. Mr. Lu's men, or what remained of them, were being surrounded, cut off in ones and twos, slaughtered.

Susan was fiercely clutching the pommel of her saddle. She was shivering with cold, with fatigue, with terror. She could still hear that soft, icy whisper of Mr. Lu, she said, as he uttered those hideous things.

"I wanted to kill that woman!" she gasped. "What had Bill done? He hadn't harmed any one! He was one of the finest men that ever lived! Yet I couldn't kill her. She did love him, Peter. She was simply mad about him. But she had to kill him!"

They pushed on. Peter had only a vague idea where the power plant was, in relation to this valley. He believed that it was situated in a northeasterly direction. They would strike north until they reached the lake. This they could follow eastward to the dam.

THE MOON HAD set by the time they reached the lake, and they were still five or six miles from the construction camp. Peter's plan was to stop only long enough there for fresh horses and provisions to suffice them for the two-hundred-mile trip over hills and desert to the village of Len Ying, where Dr. Hang would take them in. But they would not remain in Len Ying longer than a day. They must leave China forever, and as quickly as possible.

It was almost dawn when the two fugitives reached the dam. Peter dismounted there to reconnoiter. In the darkness below the dam he saw lights burning in the company shacks. Farther down the river, where a temporary village

had been built to house the labor gangs, more lights twin-
kled. Distantly he heard the brazen clang of cymbals.

But the camp looked peaceful enough. Leaving the
horses beside the lake, he helped Susan across the dam
and down the path to the camp. She was physically and
nervously exhausted. All of her customary jauntiness had
deserted her. She was cold and shaking with fright. The
world had suddenly become a menacing place. She whispered over and over that it was all her fault. If she had kept
silent, if she had not let that madman bully her into talking,
none of this would have happened. And Peter's denials
that this was so were useless. Susan was on the verge of
collapse. He did not see how she could possibly undertake
that arduous journey to Len Ying.

21

THE FLOOD

THE FIRST FULL saffron glow of morning was riding the eastern ranges when the man and the girl reached Lee Gow's shack. The young Chinese engineer opened the door and stared at them. His face was the color of lead. Nor did it lighten when he saw who his visitors were. Dully, he stared at them.

Peter's tired smile vanished from his lips. There was a candle burning on the table behind Lee Gow. On matting on the floor beside the table lay Lee Gow's wife and his three-months-old daughter. Their eyes were open, vacantly, glassily staring.

His wife and child, Lee Gow quietly explained, were victims of that first rain of bullets which Mr. Lu's men had poured into the camp when they crept up from their sampan flotilla to slaughter Strang's forces and to capture Peter and Bill Montgomery. Lee himself had been spared.

Peter knew that he was sick with grief and despair, yet his voice was calm. Only his dull eyes, his leaden color, betrayed the extent, the depth of his woe.

Quietly he made his report. Of the eight hundred labor coolies living in the village, forty-eight were dead, and seventy-nine were injured, seventeen fatally. Among the score of engineers and foremen, the toll had been lighter. Two men were dead; three were seriously wounded; one would die. Of the two men dead, one was Li Fong Chang, the concrete boss.

"But I have had the electricians working," said Lee Gow, "and I have worked myself most of the night, Mr. Moore. Everything is in readiness. Today, I believe, was the day when we must begin delivering current to Dr. Hang Win, in order to fulfill the terms of the contract."

Peter heard his assistant's voice, but scarcely knew what he was saying. Once again, he was numbed by a wave of cold, murderous fury. Mr. Lu had, as if with his own hands, murdered Mrs. Lee Gow and her tiny daughter. He had coldly ordered the murder of Bill Montgomery. The ruthless, annihilating monster behind that cold soft whisper had casually done all this.

Susan was gripping Peter's arm. He could feel the pressure of her fingernails. Since uttering a faint cry of horror at seeing the dead woman and her dead infant, Susan had said nothing. Now she said, listlessly, "Peter.—What is going to happen?"

"I am taking you to Len Ying."

"You haven't changed your mind?"

He shook his head. He knew what was behind that question—a deeper question. Was he going to do absolutely nothing about the Blue Scorpion's monstrous brutality? Wasn't he, somehow, going to strike back?

Strike back at what?—These mountains? The sky? They were still under the sinister shadow of that inhuman thinking machine. If they got out with their lives, they would be very fortunate. They might devote the remainder of their

lives, if they made good their escape, to striking back.—
But not now. Not yet!

Susan had turned away from the door. Peter heard a
muffled sound, like the distant shouting of many men.
Then Susan cried, "Peter! They're coming again!—Up the
river!"

Peter backed out of the doorway.

PERHAPS A MILE away they were, those sampans. The
river was choked with them. Scores of them—hundreds
of them! All swarming black with men. An armada of
sampans driving up the river!

That glimpse was so startling that for a moment Peter
could neither move nor speak. His assumption had
evidently been correct: Mr. Lu's forces had camped down
the river, where the gorge was wider. Some of them had
come to put down Dr. Strang's invaders, and these had
followed behind the horsemen, to guard the Charcoal
Pagoda.

The remainder were now coming up the river. Had they
been apprised by some fugitive that Mr. Lu's forces had
been slaughtered? Or had Mr. Lu directed them here? It
was likely that they were acting under orders to search the
camp for Peter and Susan, to comb the surrounding hills
if they did not find them there.

The amber light of dawn gleamed through pale mists on
the flailing sweeps. Obviously, these new invaders expected
no resistance, or they would not have risked coming by
the river.

Near the spot where Susan and Peter stood, a crowd of
men, gang bosses, installation men and coolies, were gathering in the cheerless light.

Peter asked Lee Gow if the penstock gate had been raised. The Chinese engineer said that it had been raised some hours ago. "There is water in the penstock," he added.

Peter said sharply, "Lee Gow, take these men down and open the wicket gates!—Susan, you can help me."

Lee Gow, followed by the men, went down into the power house to work the hand wheels with which the wicket gates were opened or closed. Peter and Susan went into the control room and waited. It would take several minutes for those ponderous steel gates to be open. When there was power on the line, it would be possible to open or close them in a matter of seconds.

The windows in the control room looked down upon the river. Through the dawn mists, the sampan armada could be seen. But it was no longer a ghostly armada. The sky, growing brighter, revealed men clustered in the bow of every boat. Light flickered on steel.

Peter nervously walked back and forth between the windows and the switchboard. And suddenly he saw a fleck of white foam out on the river, beyond the tail-race from the turbine. Then another. Then the arching of a wave.

He ran to the switchboard and closed the excitation breaker, then the field breaker. He watched the voltmeter. It was beginning to climb. He ran back to the windows. It would take some time for that massive machine to build up speed.—But the water in the river was beginning to churn. A foaming white plume appeared in the tail-race. He ran back to the switchboard, and when he returned to the window, the white plume had swollen, had become a roaring jet of water, yards in diameter.

BACK AGAIN TO the switchboard.—The voltmeter needle

had climbed to ten thousand—ten thousand volts. Only three thousand more—It swung up to eleven thousand.

Susan cried excitedly, above the vibration of the mighty machine, "Peter!—Quick!"

He ran back to the window. The tail-race was now a churn of white foam. The turbine's roar ceased to rise; it steadied, settled to a persistent note. It had reached top speed; the governor was holding it at that speed.

But Peter was not thinking of the governor now. With a grim smile, he was watching the river and those sampans. Water was boiling out through the tail-race now, at the rate of more than a hundred million cubic feet per minute. The other turbine would soon be discharging an equal amount.

He saw the first toppling wave reach the vanguard of sampans, saw the first of the boats overturn in the whirling froth. It rolled over and over, collided with another sampan.

Peter wished that he could have trapped them in the tail-race. Then the annihilation of Mr. Lu's hosts would have been complete. But he had accomplished his object; he had changed the river from a placid stream to a boiling torrent. Water was surging through the gorge at twenty miles an hour.

The sampans were in a hopeless tangle. In an interval of seconds, they were wedged in solid formation from one side of the gorge to the other. Another tidal wave drove down on them. Peter saw men and boats vanish under a smother of white water. Then the tangled mass was swept downstream.

Grimly watching the churning race of the water, strewn with men and litter from the overturned boats, Peter said, "Our system of generating current may be crude and wasteful, as Mr. Lu says. Certainly, we can't hold this machine—or any part of it—in the palm of one hand. But it does seem to give us a certain advantage."

He took Susan by the arm and led her to the switchboard. The voltmeter registered thirteen thousand.

"Press that button," he said.

Susan pressed the button. The switchboard glowed with light. Sixty thousand volts surged on the transmission line.

Peter Moore took Susan in his arms and kissed her. Then he said, "You and I are through with China!—We're going away—and we're never coming back. We're through with adventure."

Susan smiled. It was a mysterious little smile. "Where are we going?"

"Does it matter?" Peter said.

THE MASTER MAGICIAN

*Peter the Brazen was promised an interesting
death—by one of the Orient's master minds*

1

IN THE DARK

ICE HOUSE LANE has always been a dark, dangerous little thoroughfare—the scene of quiet knifings innumerable. The nearest street lamp is well up the hill and around the bend, where Duddel and Zetland and Wyndham Streets and Albert Road, after twisting and writhing about among the hills, triumphantly merge.

Ice House Lane is a lonely little lane at best. It climbs steeply from Queen's Road and quickly loses itself in the hill that sweeps up so majestically from Hong Kong Harbor. Its unimportance is frowned upon by dingy houses and frowzy establishments. Here are obscure merchants and traders who deal in third-rate opium and camphor and ginger.

Here, too, is Ice House Inn, a very obscure inn, which commends itself to the wayfarer because of its very obscurity and many exits. In Ice House Inn a hunted man may rest his weariness, secure in the knowledge that he can make escape, if necessary, by any of thirteen exits.

Peter Moore had selected Ice House Inn as a temporary abode, while his enemies in northern China forgot his existence, entirely because of its obscurity and its handy exits. He came and went very quietly, generally after dark. He did

A scene was appearing in the crystal!

not relish the dankness and furtive air of Ice House Inn. But dankness and furtiveness are preferable to six inches of steel in the back.

Turning the corner into Ice House Lane on this particular night, he was totally unprepared for the surprise that awaited him. He collided with a stranger in the dark.

It was darker at that corner than the innermost passage in a Chinese Emperor's tomb, darker than the inside of a cow. Sometimes there was light from the stars. Tonight there were no stars. Salty vapor was rolling in from the sea, and at higher altitudes this vapor formed billowing dark clouds.

There was no good reason to suppose that the collision was not an innocent accident. Afterward, Peter Moore realized that the fellow must have been waiting there. There was a thump as the two men met. And while Moore could see nothing of him, his groping hands informed him that the man was heavy and muscular—a white man in white man's clothing.

Both men grunted, then laughed, then apologized. Moore's groping hand encountered the man's hand. On the instant, the hand of the invisible stranger slipped a small flat object into his hand. And he was promptly gone.

Peter Moore yelled after him, and started to follow. But he heard no footsteps or echoes of footsteps. He ran all the way back to Queen's Road. A ricksha coolie went clop-clopping down the moist pavement between the shafts of his empty vehicle. Against a moldy brick wall, a Sikh in a dirty red turban was broiling a fragment of fish at the end of chopsticks over the glowing coal of a brazier.

The American ran back to the intersection. He peered into doorways, into likely lurking places. But the man with whom he had collided was nowhere to be seen.

Having satisfied himself that search was useless, he stepped into a deep doorway, made sure that he was unobserved, and struck a match. In the light of the match flame, he scrutinized the object which had been thrust into his hand by the mysterious stranger.

It looked at first like a thin, flat, red candy lozenge, about an inch square.

But the little red lozenge, unfolded, became a sheet of crackling red paper, similar to the paper in which, with tinfoil, camera films are wrapped. The match flame showed a row of tiny manikins drawn in white ink. There were five of them. Each was the symbol of a man. The three symbols at the left of the row were checked off.

Moore studied this unsigned cryptograph with eyes at first surprised and wondering, then incredulous. The flame of the match, forgotten, burned down to his fingers. He dropped the stub of the match, thrust the red paper into his pocket and went up the hill to Ice House Inn at a lope.

In the dark and unwholesome reception room was an old-fashioned wall telephone. He nervously called a number. A man answered. Moore asked for Miss Susan O'Gilvie.

A clear, crisp young voice presently sounded in Moore's ear. When he spoke, Miss O'Gilvie gave a little shriek of delight.

"I've changed my mind," he said. "Do you still want to go to Roger Pennekamp's party?"

"I'd love to! I'm dying to!" she cried. Then, in a hushed voice, she added, "Has anything happened?"

"No," he said.

A LEAN GRAY shape like a starved rat slunk out between two blobs of darkness which were fishing junks. It was a motor launch, low, lean, powerful. It was running without lights of any kind.

It crept out of the vaporous dark, whispered past under the glossy white stern of the yacht Buccaneer and slipped off in the direction of Hung-bom Bay, picking its way among the rusty-sided tramps and the sleeping sampans and junks with which Hong Kong Harbor was littered.

As it passed, the man who stood smoking a cigarette at the stern rail of the Buccaneer became aware that a pair of green eyes were steadily staring up at him from one of the portholes. Nothing but the two eyes. No face. No mouth. No nose. They might have been set in the head of a man or a leopard or a gigantic snake. They were as cold as bits of glacier ice. Sparks of sly intelligence, they stared up at the young man in the dress suit with unwinking curiosity. As the porthole passed, the eyes slowly slid in invisible sockets.

These eyes were so cold and somehow so sinister that the young man in the dress suit felt a momentary uneasiness, as if a malignant will were reaching out and coming to grips with his own; and the sensation it gave him was that he had touched some creature that was ugly and slimy.

With a flick of his fingers, he sent his cigarette spinning down through the air. The glowing ruby spark dropped into the water beside the gray launch, missing the porthole by inches and giving him a fleeting glimpse of the face in which the green eyes were set—a face oily and square, the color of saffron.

Peter Moore had expected to recognize that face, but he was sure that he had never seen it before.

He watched the gray launch slink and vanish into the thin mist with a babbling of exhaust from throttled engines, and he made sure once again that the automatic pistol in the holster strapped under his left armpit was there.

He was not aware that a Chinese deckhand had crept up behind him on silent felt soles and had held up two fingers of one yellow hand for the green eyes to see. Nor was he yet quite aware that the gray launch might prove to be the herald of an amazing adventure.

But he was suspicious.

Dance music, as soft and smooth as though filtered through silk, came from the Buccaneer's ballroom, to mingle with the creakings and groanings of the shipping anchored and moored all about. Scents of expensive perfumes, too, mingled with the stench from these ageless hulks.

Roger Pennekamp was giving this party with his customary lavishness. There were over a bundled guests aboard—the cream of Hong Kong's diplomatic and social circles. The Recourse Bay Hotel orchestra bad been hired for the evening. There was an abundance of food and anything you wished to drink, from good German beer to vintage champagne.

Peter Moore was by way of being the guest of honor—a very belated guest of honor. Roger Pennekamp had sailed into "The Pearl of the Orient" this morning in his palatial yacht, had ferreted out Peter Moore and insisted on celebrating their reunion. They hadn't met in six years.

"I'm taking a took around the world, studying conditions," the American oil millionaire had explained, "and when I heard the rumor, in Singapore, that you were back in southern China, I came two thousand miles out of my way to say hello."

But there was more than that behind the Buccaneer's visit. There was trouble. Peter Moore had detected it in the eyes of his old friend. They were the eyes of a man haunted by fear.

Moore now understood why. The lozenge of red paper explained why—with shocking eloquence.

He had been opposed to the party because he was systematically avoiding all social functions. He was living according to a Confucian proverb: What the eye does not see and the ear does not hear, the brain does not concern itself with.

His determination to avoid being seen in public had been shattered by the little crackling sheet of red paper. With troubled eyes on the mist into which the gray launch had slipped, he heard a girl's low, excited voice say, "Peter! The next dance is ours! Remember!"

HE TURNED TO find Susan, her eyes bright, her face pink with excitement, her dark sleek hair disarrayed. When she was excited she was beautiful.

Her new gown, of midnight-blue satin, was cleverly cut to reveal the beauty of her slim tanned shoulders and practically her entire and equally beautiful slim back. The matched pearls about her neck seemed to glow with inner fires against the rich golden brown of her skin.

There was something very warm, very vital, about Susan O'Gilvie. Moore had never seen the pearls before. They must be worth a quarter of a million. He would perhaps never see them again. He sometimes suspected Susan of wearing jewels once, then giving them away.

Once, a pair of diamond heels she had worn had almost cost both of them their lives. She scorned his warning that to wear costly jewels in China was to invite death. In fact, she scorned warnings of any nature.

Reputed to be the richest young woman in America, if not in the world, she could afford to indulge her whims.

Susan was a thrill hunter—a girl with an insatiable hunger for adventurous excitement.

Time after time she had plunged herself into dangerous predicaments and had frantically called upon Peter Moore to help. Since the eventful night of their meeting on the Transpacific crossing, she had—always with the most innocent of intentions—drawn him into one dangerous Oriental complication after another, until he was now a hunted man, a refugee. It was as if she had deliberately spun a web of enchantment about the young man, a web with threads of gold. But he was not in love with Susan O'Gilvie.

Looking at her vivid loveliness now, he told himself so emphatically. He could not possibly love a girl with her thirst for excitement, her greed for thrills, and he certainly could not love a girl whose weekly income was greater than his yearly salary from the General Electric Company.

Yet her attitude, even when she was angry with him, was that he had always belonged to her, and always would.

Her eyes, not blue, but a deep, alluring violet, were trying to transmit an appeal, a message. She said, menacingly, almost growling it, "Remember! This is our dance!"

Moore looked about for an explanation. He suspected that she was up to more mischief. Then he saw the cause of her perturbation—a tall, slim, black-haired young man who was forging through a group of men and women near a doorway.

Jason Whitelaw had become, in the past month, something of a problem. He was the latest of Susan's endless procession of lovesick young men. Jason Whitelaw was taking a sightseeing trip through the Far East when, in

Hong Kong, he had met Susan—and condensed his sight-seeing.

He was a cultured, suave young man from Boston, and he appeared to have an independent income. Susan treated him coldly; gave him no encouragement. She had been a target for too many fortune hunters.

It seemed to Peter Moore that Jason Whitelaw was eminently eligible, but when he said so to Susan, she had indignantly cried: "Stop throwing eligible young men at me! When I get around to thinking of marriage, you are going to be the victim. Besides, I think Jason Whitelaw is snaky."

He didn't, as he approached now, look snaky to Peter. He looked like a hurt and crestfallen young man. His dark eyes were liquidly appealing.

Susan, backing to the rail beside Peter, slipped her hand through his arm and seemed to snuggle against him.

"Mr. Moore asked me for this dance," she said sweetly.

The black-haired young man looked imploringly at Peter, and Peter, feeling very sorry for him, said, "We're going to sit it out. You'd better join us."

He winced as Susan pinched his arm. Then she quickly said, "Jason, I've lost my scarf. Will you see if I left it in the bows?"

Jason Whitelaw hesitated. He looked suspicious and even more hurt, as if he knew that she was merely trying to get rid of him.

"Will you wait here?" he said in his deep, melancholy voice.

"Of course we will!" Peter said heartily.

When the sorrowful young man had gone, Susan sighed

impatiently. "He makes me furious! He's so damned meek! He said he'd jump off a dock with a piece of railroad iron tied to his neck if I didn't promise to marry him. I said I'd help him tie it on! It was dark and spooky up there. He tried to kiss me. It was like being kissed by a dying calf. And what's more," she said, working herself into a fine fury, "I'm going to do something violent to you if you tell me once more to be nice to him. I'm a one-man woman. And I've worn myself to a shadow being nice to him. I despise him!"

MOORE CHUCKLED. SUSAN indignantly removed her hand from his arm and stared balefully across the black water toward the lights of the Peak. The reflections of these lights on the misty water were dull blades like disused swords.

Susan shivered and, looking up contritely, said, "I'm sorry I got mad, Peter. But the truth is, I feel uneasy. I've had a premonition all evening that something ugly is going to happen."

Peter nodded, with a lazy grin.

"Yeah?" he drawled. "You're up to something, and you're breaking it gently."

"Not at all, my dear," she said crisply. "Ever since you telephoned me, I've felt uneasy. And I wish you would explain why you changed your mind about coming to this party."

A man's deep voice interrupted her with, "I hope I'm not intruding." It was their host. Roger Pennekamp was a heavy-set man of about fifty-five, with the keen eyes, the powerful chin and the executive manner which are commonly ascribed to American business giants.

He gave Susan an admiring smile, but looked at Peter grimly. "Pete," he said, "it's time for us to go into a huddle. I've got something on my mind that won't keep any longer. Let's go to my room where we can have privacy and I'll tell you my real reason for barging up to Hong Kong to see you."

Susan started impulsively away, but the oil magnate said quickly, "No, no, Miss O'Gilvie. You're included. You're a clever young woman, and you may be helpful. It is a very disturbing mystery. We'll need your level head."

Susan darted a somewhat triumphant look at Peter as Mr. Pennekamp took her arm. She had seldom been accused of being level-headed, and she was seldom taken so seriously. She was flattered.

Moore followed them up the wide deck to the owner's suite. The door was opened upon an airy, spacious sitting room, as luxurious as the drawing room of an expensive apartment. Shelves along the walls were inviting with books. There was even a fireplace in which were firedogs supporting halved logs ready to be kindled.

Moore observed, in one corner, a low ebony taboret inlaid with mother-o'-pearl on which stood a carved ebony elephant. On the tusks and trunk reposed a sphere of crystal about four inches in diameter, as clear as a drop of rain water. He recalled that Roger Pennekamp had always been interested in occult phenomena, and he remembered that Roger Pennekamp had, in the old days, consulted a crystal ball. This one betrayed the value he placed on metaphysical paraphernalia. It was a museum piece, worth a small fortune.

Closing and bolting the door, the American millionaire said harshly, "Pete, I learned in Singapore that Hiram Coopwood vanished two months ago!"

Susan glanced quickly at Peter Moore. His eyes were lazily closed. He looked as if he were grinning. He wasn't grinning. It was a queer expression, instantly gone.

"Two of us left," he said quietly.

The millionaire gravely nodded. "You and I, Pete."

Susan excitedly cried, "How perfectly fascinating!"

2

THE MENACE

ROGER PENNEKAMP TOOK a rich-looking blond cigar from a bronze humidor, bit off the end and lit it. His hand holding the match was trembling a little. Susan did not miss that detail, or that he looked pale and haggard.

He said, "Did you get one of these?"

And he removed from his vest pocket a little lozenge of red paper, similar to the one which the mysterious stranger had thrust into Moore's hand in the dark of Ice House Lane. It proved, when he unfolded it, to be identical. There were the five little figures of men, in white ink, with the three on the left checked off.

Moore nodded, and removed the cryptograph from his pocket.

"You didn't even mention it," Susan said indignantly. "What does it mean?"

"The five figures," Mr. Pennekamp replied, "stand for five men. The three that are checked off are John Kyle, Adam Brumpter, and Hiram Coopwood. The two unchecked figures are Peter and myself. John Kyle, Adam Brumpter and Hiram Coopwood are checked off because they have one by one vanished. John Kyle disappeared in 1927 while prospecting for gold in New Zealand. Adam Brumpter vanished from a hotel in Buitenzorg, Java, in 1929. Hiram Coopwood walked out of his bungalow in Singapore one night two months ago and has not been heard from since. Pete, has anything happened to you?"

"Nothing so far."

"Then I must be slated for the next disappearance. Within the last few months, three attempts have been made. In Zanzibar, an ivory trader who happened to bear a close resemblance to me was murdered. He was my dinner guest. We were sitting in the stern with the lights out because of the mosquitoes. I went to fetch some fresh cigars. When I returned, he was gone. Next morning his body was found floating in the harbor, with a brass wire around his neck.

"In Ceylon, two Hindus were shot by members of my crew while attempting to pick the lock of that door. They were shot because, since these things began to happen, I've given orders to my crew to shoot first and ask questions afterward.

"In Sydney, a definite kidnap attempt was made. I was walking down a dark street, on my way to the waterfront from a hotel. Four men jumped me—threw a black cloak over my head. By pure luck, a policeman happened along; they whisked off the cloak—vanished!"

Susan uttered a small shriek. She looked excitedly from Pennekamp to Moore. She fired questions: "But why? What's at the bottom of it? What have you done? Who sent this message?"

"Zarlo."

"Who?" Susan bleated.

The millionaire looked surprised. "Hasn't Pete told you about Zarlo?"

"No!"

"It was a closed book," Peter said grimly. "I hoped it would stay closed."

"But who," Susan panted, "is Zarlo?"

"A human mystery," Pennekamp replied. "The most dangerous individual in the Far East. A sorcerer. A magic worker—black magic! A master of the occult. A hypnotist. A mind reader. The only white man I ever knew who had thoroughly mastered the mysteries of Yoga. A man who can, with the crystal ball, twist your mind inside out— make you completely the slave of his will!"

Susan glanced quickly at Peter. She knew that he did not believe in such things. But Susan was always ready to believe anything that sounded thrilling.

She said breathlessly, "He sounds positively fantastic! He doesn't sound human!"

"He doesn't," Pennekamp said, "look human. He's tall, lean and dark. Black cavernous eyes. A bony skull. The most sinister looking man I've ever seen."

"Why does he want you and Peter to vanish?"

"We offended him," said Peter.

"We kicked him off a throne," Pennekamp amplified.

"And let a wild mob kick him around in the dust," Peter added with a wry grin.

Susan expelled her breath with an explosive sound "Tell me about it!" she commanded.

"IT HAPPENED," THE millionaire said, "about six years ago in the sultanry of Tuzpan, in Luzon. Four of us—four Americans—were involved. I had an oil concession, John

Kyle a copra concession, and Hiram Coopwood and Adam Brumpter, respectively, a tin mine and a gold mine."

"None of us was in Tuzpan when the trouble started—when Zarlo came to Tuzpan. Why he went there or where he came from no one knows. I heard a strange rumor that a white man—a tall, sinister white man—had become the king of Tuzpan.

"It didn't make sense. Tuzpan was ruled by a native girl, Queen Lali, the daughter of old Sultan Malava. Zarlo came to Tuzpan, evidently saw rich opportunities, and promptly dominated Lali's will.

"His first act was to order all Americans out of the sultanry. Actually, Queen Lali issued that ukase. Tuzpan, being in the Philippines, is supposed to be an American protectorate, and I don't have to mention the sinfully careless policy of the United States in dealing with her protectorates. She lets those old Philippine sultans do very much as they please.

"Zarlo did exactly as he pleased. What he wanted, apparently, was a clear field for practicing a fanatical religion. It was a horrible religion. It involved human sacrifice and bloodletting for the supposed purification of the soul. Briefly, his idea was general moral degradation. He was, of course, to be the god."

"He must have been mad," Susan said.

"No," Pennekamp disagreed, "he was only shrewd. There was something back of that religious idea. I mean, it was part of some plan. God knows what the plan was."

The millionaire mopped perspiration from his forehead with a billowing white handkerchief.

"He was such a striking devil. That was it! He did look

like the devil—like the conventional portraits you've seen of Satan. All he lacked was horns. He had the deep-set eyes, the satanic smile, and he certainly had the devil's persuasiveness—and dark powers.

"When the Tuzpan trouble started, I was in Japan with John Kyle. I cabled Pete, in Shanghai, to go down and investigate. Because Pete has a greater practical knowledge of the Far East than any white man out here.

"Pete hadn't been in Tuzpan ten hours when Zarlo ordered his arrest. Pete escaped through the jungles, made his way to Manila and cabled me his information. I chartered a tramp steamer, picked up Brumpter and Coopwood in Hong Kong, and Pete in Manila. We went to Tuzpan.

"We went ashore—the five of us—armed to the teeth. It's always been my rule, in a surprise attack, to strike fast and hard. We struck hard. We went to the palmetto house where Zarlo was holding court—actually sitting on a throne—and before any one realized what we were up to, we unthroned Zarlo. I mean, we pulled and kicked him off his teakwood throne!

"The mob that had followed us from the waterfront and through the streets waited for lightning to strike us for our effrontery to the Great White God. But the only lightning striking that afternoon was in Pete's oratory.

"He used the throne as a soap-box. He made a speech in the native dialect while we held Zarlo. The mob seemed hypnotized."

"What," Susan breathlessly interrupted, "did you say to them, Peter?"

Moore grinned. "It began," he said: " 'Friends, Tuzpanians and countrymen, lend me your ears. I come to bury Zarlo, not to praise him!'"

"You make me furious," Susan said. "Go on, Mr. Pennekamp."

"Whatever it was Pete said, it calmed them down. But it was a dangerous calm. They suddenly decided that Zarlo had tricked them. Before we could interfere, they ganged him.

"Mind you, we didn't want that. We didn't want his life. We simply wanted him to clear out of Tuzpan, and we were using the most effective method we knew. But it was too effective. Things were out of control—wild!

"They dragged him out of our hands. They tore off his clothes. They stoned him. They kicked him around in the dirt. He got away finally, in a dugout. But before he went, he sent us his compliments. He said he would get us all!

"We'd heard too many down-and-outers make such threats to worry. We forgot Zarlo. Queen Lali came out of her trance and ruled Tuzpan again. Every so often, you know, some ambitious white man finds himself on the beach and cooks up the scheme of becoming king of some native tribe. Generally, they don't last long. They blow up like toy balloons. I put Zarlo in that class. And that was where I made my mistake.

"When John Kyle disappeared in New Zealand, I wasn't alarmed. He had enemies. He led a dangerous life. But when Brumpter vanished similarly in Java I was alarmed. And when Hiram Goopwood vanished in the identical manner of the others, I knew that Zarlo—somewhere—somehow—was making good on that threat of his.

"Any lingering doubts in my mind were dismissed when

these mysterious occurrences I mentioned began happening to me. It appeared definitely that I was to be the next victim."

Susan's eyes were almost black with excitement. "But where is Zarlo?"

The oil magnate shook his head as if with weariness. And wearily said, "I don't know. No one knows. In the past two months, I've spent upwards of two hundred thousand—gold—trying to find out. I've hired the cleverest detectives in the Far East. I've had this part of the world combed for Zarlo—Japan, Mongolia, China, India, Cambodia, Malaya, the South Seas. It's no use. This minute, I'd give a cold million to know where he is!"

MR. PENNEKAMP'S CIGAR had gone out. He had chewed the end of it to shreds. He burst out savagely, "Damn him! He's laughing at me! He's playing with me! He's got me! Why do you suppose he sent this cryptograph? To show his contempt! He's failed three times, but sometime he won't fail—in spite of every precaution I can take! I can't lock myself up in a fort. I've got to keep on the go. My business demands it. And sooner or later he's going to succeed. And he's going to get you, too, Pete!"

Susan, shivering, cried, "Oh, please don't say such things! There must be some way."

Pennekamp said heavily, "I've exhausted all the ways there are. I've used the crystal. Pete laughs at such things. But I've got images in it. I know that Zarlo uses one. I know that if I just concentrate, if the vibrations are right, I can catch him by the use of the crystal.

"All right!" he shouted. "Go on and laugh!"

"I'm not laughing," Peter said.

"But you think it's a joke!"

"No. I've never been convinced. I'm willing to be convinced."

"All right. Wait until midnight. It always works best for me after midnight. I'll try to show you what I've seen every night for the past two weeks."

"The same image?"

"The same image—not clear enough to describe."

"Do you think," Susan breathed, "it has something to do with Zarlo?"

"I'm convinced of it!"

Susan looked at Peter with a certain hostility. "I suppose you don't agree with that, either."

He firmly shook his head.

"Or that Zarlo has the powers that Mr. Pennekamp says he has?"

"I don't believe that Zarlo has occult powers," Peter answered. "I concede him nothing but a tremendous personality—evil but tremendous—and powerful magnetism. And terrific will power." He grinned faintly. "You see, Susan, I'm one of the men who has never seen an Indian boy climb a rope suspended from nothing."

Susan snorted irefully. "But Mr. Pennekamp has made a study of such things. Look at those books!"

Peter had seen those books six years ago—many of them. He knew that Pennekamp had a library well stocked with works on Yoga, hypnotism, spiritism, demonology, crystal-gazing, mind reading, thought transference, astrology and kindred subjects. Many of them Peter had studied.

"I suppose," Susan said, "that you don't think Zarlo used

magical powers of some kind in making those three men vanish!"

Again Peter shook his head. "No, Susan. My humble opinion, since you've asked for it, is that Zarlo is comfortably entrenched, hidden, somewhere, and has sufficient means to pay handsomely for mysterious disappearances. But don't think that I underestimate his mentality. I simply believe that he is the brains, the so-called master mind, behind a very efficient organization."

Susan said stubbornly, "I think you're wrong. I agree absolutely with Mr. Pennekamp." And she looked at Mr. Pennekamp with shining eyes. Always, when given the choice, Susan decided on whatever would give her the greatest thrill.

The millionaire said, "Frankly, Pete, I came up here because I want to place myself in your hands. I want you to take charge of this horrible mess. I'll place unlimited funds at your disposal. The Buccaneer will go wherever you say. Only stay aboard. Match your wits with Zarlo's. I must return to my guests now. Don't go ashore tonight until I've given you the crystal demonstration. It may give us a clew of some sort."

Some one tapped discreetly at the bolted door. Peter, who was nearest, unbolted and opened it.

Jason Whitelaw was standing outside with Susan's black-and-silver scarf draped over one arm. His eyes were liquidly appealing.

Beyond him, beyond the rail, Peter saw the gray launch sliding past, vanishing into the vaporous murk between the two junks.

3

KIDNAPED

SUSAN SAID, IN a voice of exasperation, "Oh, Lord."

"I thought you were going to wait," the sad-eyed young man said reproachfully. "You said you would."

Susan caught a sharp glance from Peter and said, "I'm awfully sorry, Jason, but I forgot all about it."

"You promised me another dance," Jason said mournfully, "and the orchestra is playing 'Good Night, Ladies.'"

Susan glanced again at Peter, a little uncertainly. His eyes said very plainly, "Be a good sport." And hers flashed back the equally plain retort, "I'm just fed up with being nice to him!"

But she went, thereby proving that Peter Moore exercised some slight control over that spirited young person.

A group of guests came up the deck, heading for this doorway. Among them Peter recognized Henshaw, the American consul to Hong Kong. Peter was not precisely on speaking terms with Consul Henshaw. Consul Henshaw had made it very clear, in a brief conversation less than one week ago, that Peter Moore's continued presence in Hong Kong was highly undesirable. And it seemed to Peter, at that moment, that American consuls, in cities up and down the China coast, had been murmuring such messages to him ever since he was a little boy.

He slipped out on deck. He wanted to keep an eye on that gray launch. And he wanted to be alone, to think.

The deck was almost deserted. The party was rapidly breaking up. A launch loaded with guests was just leaving the ship's ladder for Blake Pier. The orchestra, sobbing out "Good Night, Ladies," sounded as if it were dying.

Peter made his way up to the boat deck. From here he could see the harbor better. A square white excrescence amidships—just abaft the yellow funnel—he presumed was the wireless shack. It was dark. He tried the doorknob. Locked.

An amiable voice said, "Homesick, Mr. Moore?"

A tall, slender young man was lounging against a funnel guy. In the glow from the wheelhouse, Peter discerned a small black mustache in a hard, brown face, and the mild gleam of gold on collar and sleeves. The captain.

"My name's Tackaberry. I've seen you around. You used to be a wireless operator, didn't you, before you stood the coast on its ear?"

Peter Moore was always emphatic in his denials that he was a trouble hunter. He maintained that his escapades were always innocent enough, but his reputation was a case of the dog once given a bad name. It stuck.

But he wasn't feeling argumentative. Captain Tackaberry detached himself from the funnel guy and said, "I suppose the old man has called you in to help ride herd."

Peter wasn't giving out information, either. "Where did he sign you on?"

"Sydney. Or are you replacing Sparks?"

"No," said Peter. "I'm just prowling around, wondering about a gray launch I've seen standing off and on out there."

"Her?" the skipper said. "Isn't she a police boat?"

"No. The harbor police boats are black and carry an antenna. I'd keep an eye on her."

He had the feeling, as he continued aft, that the air was charged with a "Says you!" Captain Tackaberry was cocky, and, by the bulk at his hip, he was, Peter gathered, armed. Starting down an iron ladder into the stern, he reflected that Roger Pennekamp had no doubt turned his crew into an armed guard.

Reaching the main deck again, he started forward on the starboard side, watching the lights of Causeway Bay through the thin mist. He saw nothing of the gray launch.

The yacht had a deserted feeling. All the guests had left.

AT THE FORWARD turn of the deck he almost collided with Jason Whitelaw, hurrying around from the other side. Susan's black-and-silver cloak hung over one arm. He looked surprised. He said sharply, "Where's Susan?"

"I thought you took her off to dance."

"I did! But when the music stopped she told me to get her cloak and meet her at Pennekamp's cabin. She said she was going there for you. She isn't there!"

Peter wasn't alarmed. "She's probably in the engine room," he said, "kidding the engineers, or in the pantry, having a sandwich. She'll turn up."

A wild scream put a period, so to speak, to that. It came from aft and was suddenly muffled.

Peter had heard Susan cry out in terror before. He knew the sound of her scream. He saw now that the stern was in darkness.

Jason cried, "Some one just switched those lights off! It's swarming with coolies!"

Peter, starting down the deck, could see figures churning about in the semi-darkness back there.

He shouted, "Susan!" and started to run.

Roger Pennekamp, suddenly emerging from a corridor doorway, white with panic, cried, "What is it, Pete?"

"They've got Susan!" Peter, snatching out his automatic, ran on.

Just beyond the stern rail he saw the upper works of the gray launch. Two dim shapes at the rail were passing down what looked like a long, slim bundle into hands reaching up ghostlike from below.

The bundle was squirming and kicking.

He dared not fire yet. Jason, pounding down the deck beside him, panted, "Shoot! For God's sake, shoot!"

But Peter didn't shoot until the squirming bundle had vanished. His intention was to shoot his way to the rail, then to shoot into the engine compartment of the gray launch.

But his plan was frustrated. A mass of yellow men came charging toward him. Peter fired with deliberation. At his left elbow another pistol was roaring. More feet came pounding down the deck. Other feet were pounding overhead.

Then he was surrounded. His assailants were harbor *fokies*—the yellow scum of the Hong Kong waterfront, half-naked, silent, armed with knives.

He emptied the pistol into them, then clubbed it and systematically hammered heads and faces and hands.

He found himself shoulder to shoulder with Captain

Tackaberry. On his other side was Jason Whitelaw. Mr. Pennekamp was not to be seen.

The captain was wielding a revolver that looked, as its butt came clanking down on a skull, two feet in length.

Reinforcements came surging aft down both sides of the deck.

Harbor coolies were spilling over the rail like rats. Some of them reached the deck or the cabin roof of the gray launch. Others fell into the water and yelled.

A fist or knee caught Peter full and hard in his solar plexus. His breath and all desire to stand erect departed with a painful grunt.

He rolled over and tried to sit up. But his muscles were paralyzed. He could neither speak nor move.

Jason Whitelaw was a few feet away on his knees, with blood gushing out of a cut below his left eye.

The deck was littered with casualties, most of them yellow. Just behind Peter lay Roger Pennekamp, face down, clawing at the deck with his fingernails.

Some one turned on the lights as Peter got to his feet, with his breath painfully sobbing in his throat. He stiffened himself against an impulse to collapse. He wedged himself between two men at the rail who were yelling and firing into the mist with revolvers. He caught a glimpse of the gray launch vanishing into the vapors.

It disappeared with a muffled roar of powerful engines toward the open sea.

4

IN THE CRYSTAL

PETER MOORE, RECOVERING his wind, heard Captain Tackaberry profanely barking orders. He discovered that the left sleeve of his coat was slit from shoulder to elbow, that the shirt sleeve under it was slit and soaked with blood from a knife slash of which he had been unaware.

The Buccaneer was to up-anchor and get under way immediately.

It was useless. Peter knew it was useless. There was only one possible hope. He pushed himself away from the rail and staggered to the iron ladder which ran to the boat deck. He was still painfully short of breath. He laboriously climbed the ladder and made his way to the wireless house. He braced his back against the bellying side of a lifeboat and kicked until the lock gave and the door flew inward.

He turned on lights, threw switches to the transmitting position, and rapped out, with the Morse key, the call letters of the Hong Kong harbor police radio station.

When the central station answered, he tapped a message to the official in charge, briefly describing the gray launch, and requesting that it be overhauled and held with every one on board. He signed the message "Pennekamp."

Through the open door he heard the clanking of a heavy

chain, the sound of men running to and fro, then the vibration of powerful engines.

The Buccaneer was under way. When Peter went below, the deck was crowded with harbor police officers. One of the police launches, attracted by the shooting, had come alongside to investigate.

The captain of the police boat wanted the Buccaneer to remain at her anchorage for an official inquiry. Roger Pennekamp was expostulating. The yacht was meanwhile picking her way through shipping.

Peter had no interest in that argument. He was sick with worry. He was furious at himself for having let Susan out of his sight.

Returning to the wireless cabin, he put on the ear phones and waited for an answer to the message. He heard, far away, the shrill yapping of a Jap freighter talking with the Formosa station. Closer at hand were the mosquito-like voices of the harbor police boats, reporting failure. Police boats stationed in Lyeemoon Pass, Tathong Channel and Quarry Bay made their reports. No launch of the description given had been seen.

Peter went out on deck, sick with disappointment. The wrangling on the deck below was still going on. Roger Pennekamp was shouting that he didn't give a damn about British police or admiralty red tape. A cold English voice was citing a list of penalties for leaving a port without clearance papers, and for disobeying police orders.

The Buccaneer was meanwhile slipping down Tathong Channel to the sea. The lights of Kowloon dwindled.

The central police radio station was calling when Peter returned to the instruments. He wondered where the

Buccaneer's radio operator was. There was an answer to the message, and it was a disheartening answer. The gray launch, unquestionably headed for the sea, had escaped with clean heels. One of the police boats had identified and hailed it, had ordered it to halt, had sent a shot across its bows; and the gray launch had fled at a speed estimated at forty-five knots!

No one could guess where the gray launch was heading. A tramp freighter, a junk, miles offshore, might be waiting at a rendezvous to receive its passenger. Or the launch might be, at this moment, hidden behind any one of the hundreds of small and large islands with which the China coast in this region is dotted.

A Chinese boy in white appeared in the doorway and said, "That masta, him wanchee you that side." He jabbed downward with a thumb.

Peter went below. He was heartsick and still seething with self-recriminations. The police and their boat were gone. The deck had been cleared of dead and wounded. **ROGER PENNEKAMP AND** the young man from Boston were waiting for him in the sitting room of the owner's suite. Both men showed evidences of frantic worry. The millionaire was pacing up and down, chewing distractedly at a dead cigar. Jason Whitelaw was slumped in a chair, his face as white as the bandage which had been applied to the gash in his cheek.

When Peter closed the door, Pennekamp said, "I've been telling Whitelaw about Zarlo. There's no question that Zarlo was behind this attack. Those men had instructions to get the three of us—Miss O'Gilvie, you and me. They expected to overpower the crew. But we happened to strike too hard. Mark my word, Pete, this isn't the end. He'll keep on till he gets us. What have you been doing?"

Peter told him. Pennekamp nodded. "I thought you were up there. Once they got her, they were safe. And Lord knows where they're taking her!"

"To Zarlo," Peter said wearily.

Jason burst out frantically, "Good Lord, can't you find out where this fellow Zarlo is?"

Roger Pennekamp stopped pacing. "I may be able to. I think I've been on the fight track for weeks. Tonight, with so much in the air, I may have luck."

Peter realized where this was leading. The crystal ball! He knew that, in the crises of his life, Roger Pennekamp consulted that lucid sphere as some men, equally rational in all other respects, consulted astrologists, fortune tellers.

The millionaire was explaining that he could not possibly hope for results if there were skepticism or ridicule in the room. Would Peter promise to bring an open mind to the crystal. Would Whitelaw?

More to humor the distracted man than because he had the slightest faith in such things, Peter promptly assented.

"We will sit on the three sides, facing inward, facing it," Pennekamp said. "Kindly sit down, gentlemen. I will turn out all the lights save the one directly overhead."

When the two young men had seated themselves in chairs facing the crystal ball, the oil magnate switched off the lights, then pressed another button which controlled a pale green bulb overhead.

It gave a ghostly light. A pale-green spark seemed to float in the ball.

"I must ask you to help me as much as you can, gentle-men," Pennekamp said, seating himself in the third chair.

Peter, touching the table, had found that it was bolted to the deck, and that the little ebony elephant supporting the sphere was bolted, or fastened somehow, to the top of the taboret. And he supposed that this provision had been made in case of rough weather.

Pennekamp was crouched down, staring into the depths of the ball. "You must concentrate," he said tensely. "You realize that what we want to know is, where Miss O'Gil-vie is being taken. Where that is, Zarlo is. *We—must—concentrate!*"

It was not hard for Peter to concentrate. He wanted the answer to that question more than he had ever wanted anything in his life. He stared into the crystal ball until his eyes ached. It underwent, in his imagination, curious changes of substance. It became a large, perfectly round drop of water. It became a soap bubble. It became a perfect sphere of colorless transparent jelly. The reflection of the pale green light overhead played strange tricks.

He thought he saw the ball growing luminous, filled with an aurora-like display of blue and green and yellow.

Pennekamp said hoarsely, "It's coming through!"

"Blue and green and yellow!" Jason Whitelaw whispered.

Peter started. Very definitely he saw the play of light now.

The colors shifted about. The green became a horizon-tal stripe, or streak, at the bottom of the ball. Above this, golden light shimmered. And above the yellow, blue—the blue of a tropical sky.

He could not, would not, believe this. His eyes were playing tricks on him!

The blue at the top of the ball was a soft burning blue. The green at the bottom had a shivering shifting quality. He caught a glimmer of white. It shocked him. That glimmer was exactly like the frothing white of a breaking wave!

Then he saw that the glowing yellow area between sky-blue at the top and sea-green at the bottom was a cliff.

"There it comes!" Pennekamp whispered.

PETER SAW TREES now, very clearly, as if they came out of this spectroscopic fog. They were at the base of the sandstone cliff.

Now the cliff shockingly changed. It was not a cliff but a yellow skull, with sockets where the eyes had been, a socket where the nose had been.

But it wasn't a skull. It was a cliff. Blue sky overhead. Deep-green sea beneath. With a cluster of palms along the beach at the base.

Peter's heart was hammering in his ears.

"Look! Look!" Pennekamp cried harshly. "Don't you see it? The sky? The sea?"

The young man from Boston whispered, "It's there! A cliff! And palm trees!"

The millionaire said tremulously, "Pete?"

Peter said heavily, as if he were speaking in spite of himself. "Yes. It's there. Clear."

"It's what I've been seeing every night for the past two weeks!" Pennekamp said triumphantly. "But never so clear!"

Jason Whitelaw said, in a desperate voice, "Is that where she is? Is that where she is?"

"You do see it, Pete?"—a gasp.

"Yes."

"Do you make it out?" Pennekamp cried. "I mean, have you seen it before? Does it mean anything? Is it any place you've seen?"

"Wait a minute," Peter said. It was all suddenly clear—almost clear. Once, on a moonlit night, he had seen that skull-like headland.

He exclaimed, "Skull Island—Sinanga—Borneo!" as the words, or pictures, flashed into his mind.

The image was fading. The vivid, intense colors swam, dimmed. Gradually the image vanished. The ball became empty.

The green spark, a reflection of the bulb overhead, seemed to swim back out of a rainbow haze.

Roger Pennekamp sprang up, switched on the lights. His face was flushed. His eyes were glittering with excitement.

"Don't lose it!" he said with a nervous laugh, and pressed a wall button. He opened the door. When a steward appeared, he said, "Tell Captain Tackaberry to come here at once." He swung around on Peter. "Where is this place?"

"South of Borneo."

"An island?"

"A large, wild island."

"Skull Island?"

"That's what sailors call it, because of that headland. I think the name on the charts is Sinonga, or Sinanga."

Pennekamp had trotted to a wall where hung a large chart of the western Pacific. Peter joined him.

"In the Java Sea?"

"Yes, I'm sure of that—almost due west of Makassar, almost due north of Soerabaya—I'd say where the lines meet, I know it's about midway between the Equator and ten south."

They were probing about among circles and squares and oblongs on the chart—the little known islands to the south of the great irregular mass which is Borneo.

Peter found it. It was spelled Soononga.

Captain Tackaberry came in, with his white cap cocked on one side of his curly brown hair.

The owner said, "Have you ever heard of Skull Island?"

The skipper frowned, squinted, grimaced. "Yes, sir. I think so. It's familiar."

"Pete, is there any question in your mind that what you saw is the headland of Skull Island, or Soononga?"

"I'm sure."

Pennekamp jabbed his spatulate forefinger at the long rectangle labeled Soononga I.

"This is where we're going, captain. How long will it take?"

"About a week."

"Know those waters?"

"I've sailed through those islands in a windjammer. They're pretty tough waters. Bad currents."

"Well, that's where we're going. Now!"

5

SKULL ISLAND

THE NIGHT WHEN Skull Island was sighted was destined to be one of violent surprise. Roger Pennekamp, Peter Moore and Jason Whitelaw were seated in steamer chairs on the port side amidships when the excitement began.

The night was hot and still. The stars, brilliantly rippling, gleamed on a sea as flat, as dark as a sheet of slate. There was no wind except that which was created by the Buccaneer's passage. She was traveling slowly, because of uncharted reefs. At intervals a man in the bows heaved the lead and cried out the depth in fathoms to the bridge.

There was an air of tension aboard, a sense of unexpected exciting possibilities.

The three men, in deck pyjamas, were sipping long iced drinks. They spoke seldom. Out there in the darkness, they knew, was Soononga Island. Peter could all but feel the loom of it. The moon rose at a little after ten thirty. There was a forewarning silky red gleam, like ruby light shining on a taut wire, along the eastern horizon. Then the moon popped up out of the sea like a ripe red plum.

The night grew palely luminous as it rose. And as its brilliance became silver and reached out, the land they were skirting came into visibility like the image on a photo-graphic film being developed.

Far ahead, off the port bow, was the headland—a ghostly, palely-glowing thing, even at this distance and in this wan light strikingly resembling a human skull. It seemed to glow eerily, with an inward light of its own.

Peter was standing at the rail, with Jason on his left, the millionaire on his right, when it happened. Looking across the strait at the dark mystery of the island, he was wonder-ing if Susan was captive there. His face in the deck-light was haggard.

He had suddenly a curious illusion of sound. It was as if, from all around him, were the whispers of fingers, hands rubbing together.

Then the blow fell. It was, in a way, a repetition of that night in Hong Kong, more than a week ago. Suddenly, the deck was swarming with silent, half-naked men, only these invaders were dark-brown, or black—not yellow.

Before he could cry out, a hot, salty wet hand was clapped down upon his mouth, and his neck was jammed in the crook of a powerful arm.

He kicked backward, caught a shin with the heel of his foot; struck again. His captor grunted deeply, slightly relaxed that strangle hold.

Peter, writhing, twisting with all his strength, caught a blurred glimpse of men struggling all over the deck. He saw Roger Pennekamp wriggle out of a black man's arms, reach for his pistol. Day and night since Hong Kong that pistol had never been out of reach.

He fired it into the black man's mouth, and the black man went toppling back to the rail.

Peter struck out with both fists. He had the satisfaction of seeing one antagonist fall leadenly. Another. And another. But it was hopeless.

Some one dropped a black cloth down over his head. Mighty arms pinioned his arms. He was lifted. Stifling under the black hood, trying to extricate himself, he felt that he was being carried rapidly down the deck toward the stern. There were shouts and cries. Pennekamp was yelling for the crew. Evidently the invaders hadn't overpowered him.

A fist or club crashed down on Peter's head. The blow did not knock him out. It rendered him only partially unconscious. But it paralyzed his muscles, his very will to struggle. Limp, helpless, he felt himself being handed down and down.

A moment later, still held tightly by powerful hands, he heard an engine begin to purr.

More shouts and more shots.

Under him, some kind of craft gave a leap. He heard water hissing under a hull being propelled at tremendous speed.

A moment later, while his hands were held, the wrists were bound with rope, the black cloth was removed, and a strange voice said, "Take it easy, Moore."

BLINKING, HE LOOKED into the sun-blistered face of a white man with red hair. The white man sat beside him. There was a German automatic pistol in one hand. The other hand was grasping the wheel, which was of the automobile type. His face was brightly lighted from the instrument board.

The red-headed man was grinning. Peter turned his

head, looked aft. Directly aft was a covered compartment which housed the engines. Aft of the engine compartment was a large cockpit packed solid with black men—presumably the boarding party. And dwindling astern, like a vision, was the snowy white hull, with its diamond-sparkling lights, of the Buccaneer.

Some one groaned on the other side of him. He looked quickly and gave a grunt of surprise. Slumped down in a corner of the seat was the young man from Boston, wrists likewise bound. A lump over Jason's left eye looked as large as a hen's egg. He was still groggy from the blow which had raised that bump.

Peter looked back at the redhead.

"Any sense asking you questions?" he said grimly.

"Not unless you want to get hoarse," was the answer. "You better save your strength, fella."

This had a sinister sound. Peter presently learned that it had a sinister meaning.

"But you didn't get Pennekamp," he said.

"No," the redhead said harshly. "But we will. He won't leave now. He won't run out on his pals!"

The speedboat, Peter saw, was of the most modern and luxurious type. It was traveling over the smooth water of the strait at a speed of at least thirty-five knots.

He looked apprehensively toward land. Soononga Island appeared to be a solid wall of jungle growing at the foot of high dark cliffs; a sinister island, dark with sinister possibilities.

The cliff magically opened. The boat entered a zone of rich, sickly sweetness—the mingled odors of nameless jungle flowers, which, opening in the dark, were spilling their cloying sweetness into the faint breeze that drew offshore.

A river flowed out through the opening in the cliff. Beyond was a small round lake. The redhead switched on a searchlight. The boat crossed this lake with unabated speed and charged up a black river not more than twenty feet in width, arched over by the branches of trees and snakelike vines.

The tunnel thus formed echoed with the reverberations of the speedboat's exhaust. The sides of the tunnel were a tangled, slimy mass of mangrove trunks.

At a distance which Peter estimated to be approximately a mile from the lake, the redhead throttled the engines. There was a crude wharf of logs on the port side. He maneuvered the boat alongside the wharf and said curtly, "Come on, you guys."

Peter climbed out. Groaning, Jason followed. They looked about them. There was only a small clearing carved out of the jungle by the wharf—no evidences of human habitation.

"This way," the redhead said. "Step lively."

"How far?" groaned the young man from Boston.

"Plenty far."

He started ahead along a narrow trail with a flashlight in one hand. Peter observed that there were other flashlights in his pockets—one protruding from each hip pocket. They must mean a long trek.

AS THEY ADVANCED along a thin, twisting trail, which had been hacked through the jungle, the blacks began to vanish. Other trails, like tributaries, led off from it, and from time to time, a handful of the natives would slip off along one of these "feeders," presumably toward their villages.

It was a night of horror. Baleful eyes glowed at them from thickets. Insects assailed them in swarms. The trail wound and twisted through the densest jungles Peter had ever seen, through swamps, through immense fields of parched cactus grass, higher than a man's head.

Time after time, Peter stumbled over an unseen root or a slippery stone and fell. And the redhead evidently had a sense of humor. When Peter or Jason fell, the redhead laughed. He laughed when they floundered through a fast stream, waist-deep, with slimy banks tangled with alligator grass. He laughed when they cursed at unseen thorns which tore at their flesh.

The sky was filling, like a dark sphere, with the pale suffusion of tropical dawn when the three white men, followed by a half-dozen blacks, entered an immense field of the parched cactus grass. They fought their way through it, Peter judged, for a quarter of an hour. The sky was pink-stained when, reaching the other side of it, they entered another stretch of dense jungle. Monkeys chattered and shrieked at them.

The trail was well traveled here. And the night of horror came abruptly to an end. The trail ended at their objective—a towering mass of dark stone—a castle built in a clearing hewn from the jungle! It reached at least a hundred feet into the air. High up were windows. The structure had the air of an impregnable fortress.

Peter, running his eyes up the dark, moss-grown wall, reflected with sardonic humor, "Journeys end in lovers' meetings." Perhaps Susan was still alive in this grim edifice.

Knowing Zarlo, knowing how the mind of that monomaniac ran, he could picture the fate in store for him. Death by cruel torture, with Susan standing helplessly by. Zarlo had had six years in which to prepare for this triumphant moment.

They reached a heavy door of some dark tropical wood studded with the heads of bronze spikes.

The red-headed man hammered on it with the butt of his pistol. The door opened. A middle-aged man with ferret's eyes stood in a small hallway, from which a flight of stone steps ran upward. He wore the white livery of a servant in the tropics. His smile was suave and oily.

"Come in, gentlemen," he whispered.

The red-headed man was evidently not a gentleman, for he did not come in. He turned about and walked down the trail. Peter wondered where. That trail, he believed, was the only means of escape.

The man in white re-bolted the great door and said unctuously, "If you will follow me, gentlemen, I will show you your quarters."

He might have been a butler in any American or English mansion.

The two tired young men, their faces swollen from insect bites, their deck pajamas bloody and tattered from thorns and repeated falls, followed him up the stone stairway to another bronze-studded door.

He unlocked the door, and locked it after them, pocketing the key.

The hall which they had entered might have been the reception hall in any luxurious American or English country house. A living room and a library gave from it. All the floors were of a light-hued hard wood like oak. Rich oriental rugs covered them. Tapestries and fine canvases hung on the walls.

It was incredible—impossible to believe that this castle, with its luxuries, existed in the heart of a savage jungle island.

SINCE LANDING ON this island, Peter's mind had been occupied with little else but thoughts of escape, provided he could rescue Susan. Such hopes as he had were fading. As he progressed through this fantastic castle, he saw no one but the servant, yet he had the sense that his every step was sped on.

The two prisoners were conducted up a wide, handsome stairway. The bannister was of mahogany or narawood, beautifully inlaid with mother-o'-pearl.

Their escort led them down a long wide hall, with doors on either side. All were closed. Beyond each was mystery. Was Susan behind one of them?

At one of the doors the servant paused. He opened a small, pearl-handled pocket knife, and carefully cut the cords binding Jason's wrists. He gave the same service to Peter, then said, in his suave manner, "Gentlemen, you are the guests of Zarlo. Anything you wish is yours. This is your room, Mr. Whitelaw."

Jason gave Peter a bewildered look from sick, bloodshot eyes and limped into the room.

"This way, Mr. Moore."

"Don't we bunk together?"

"Hardly, sir! We have accommodations here for sixty guests and you are practically our only ones."

"Practically?"

"Practically," said the man with his unctuous smile

He had stopped at another door, six beyond Jason's.

"I am instructed to say that when you are bathed and dressed, my master has requested that you go to the green room on the floor above this. You will find clothing to fit you in the wardrobe."

With his somewhat sinister smile, he withdrew. Peter opened the door and entered a room which might have been a guest room in any rich man's house in almost any civilized country. It was tastefully, even magnificently, furnished. The furniture—bed, chairs, chest of drawers, dressing table—looked European.

Adjoining the bedroom was a luxurious bathroom in white tile. If Peter had not been so apprehensive about Susan's fate and his own future, he would have marveled at all this luxury—marveled at the patience, the money which must have been expended so lavishly to erect this remarkable retreat.

He conducted a brief tour of exploration. From two windows on one side, he looked down upon the dark green roof of the jungle. He went to the closet. It seemed to be full of men's clothes, all sizes, but not new.

Curiously, he looked in the inner coat pockets at tailors' labels, to ascertain who had worn these clothes.

A cold thrill proceeded down his spine as he read the first name. Hiram Coopwood! Hiram Coopwood, who had left his Singapore bungalow for a walk two months ago and had never been seen again! In another coat was the name of John Kyle, written in indelible ink in the label of a New York tailor. John Kyle had vanished in New Zealand in 1927. In another coat, he found the name of Adam

Brumpter, who had disappeared so mysteriously in Java in 1929.

Peter wondered why Zarlo had captured Jason. Was Jason to be an innocent victim?

All logical thought was at that moment driven from Peter's head by a sound. It was like the roar of a jungle beast, but it resembled the roar of no beast that Peter had ever heard. A snarling, half-human roar, it was blood-chilling.

Peter ran to the window. He threw it open and looked down. He saw nothing.

He had the hopeless, desperate feeling that a relentless fate was closing in on him.

6

JASON'S TRUE COLORS

THE SERVANT HAD returned to Jason Whitelaw's room. Without knocking, he turned the knob and walked in. He quickly closed the door.

The young man from Boston, exhausted, was stretched out on the bed. He sprang up now and cried hoarsely, "Where is she, Hascomb?"

The servant did not seem at all surprised that Whitelaw knew his name.

"Across the hall, sir, the third door down—left."

"Oh, my God!" the young man groaned. "Why? Why wasn't she put on another floor?"

"What difference does it make? Moore won't live long enough to bother."

Whitelaw said angrily, "That isn't the point. She must not know about him. My whole scheme is ruined if she knows he is here."

"I'm sorry, sir." Hascomb did not look sorry. He looked surly.

Impatiently, Whitelaw said, "Well, give me the key."

Hascomb forked a key out of his pocket. "I don't think you need have any alarm, Mr. Whitelaw. She is completely under the master's power."

Whitelaw snatched the key out of his hand and snapped, "Clear out of here!"

He did not wait for the door to close. He stripped off his tattered garments, ran into the bathroom and shaved and showered. Then he ran back, threw open the closet, took down a white linen suit. From a chest of drawers he removed a shirt, socks, underwear, a necktie. All these clothes fitted him perfectly.

With a glance at his bruised, swollen face in a mirror, he picked up the key and let himself out. He went to the door Hascomb had specified, inserted the key and opened it.

A girl's voice mumbled, "Peter!"

Whitelaw put his finger to his mouth, said "Sh!" warningly and closed the door. Susan got up from a chair in which she had been sitting by a window. She wore a white linen dress which obviously had not been made for her. Her face was gaunt and colorless. Her eyes had a dazed, leaden look. They were the eyes of a person drugged.

Whitelaw eagerly took her hands. She stared up at his face, blinking her eyes, as if trying hard to think.

"Jason!" she whispered. Her hands were cold and limp. She seemed inert, lifeless.

"Listen!" he said. "We must be very quiet. If I am discovered here, my life won't be worth a cent. Darling, I've come here—fought my way here through the jungles—to rescue you. I've got a ship, a schooner, waiting. Somehow, I'll get you out of here. I love you, and, if necessary, I'll die fighting for you!"

This somewhat grandiose speech did not seem to impress Susan. She was staring into his face. She whispered, thickly," Where—is he?"

"Who?"

"Peter!"

Jason averted his eyes and compressed his lips. He frowned. His shoulders seemed to sag. "In Japan," he muttered.

"Oh!" Susan said softly.

"I'm sorry, Susan. He was scared out. The night they got you in Hong Kong, he amply went all to pieces. He knew Zarlo was after him. He—he decided he would be safest in Japan."

"Peter?" the girl said incredulously. "Peter did that?"

"I'm horribly sorry. There was nothing for me to do but my best, single-handed. I found from one of the men we captured in that Hong Kong attack, where Zarlo lives. I came here. Now, listen carefully! Zarlo thinks I was ship-wrecked here. He suspects nothing. I'm going to get you out of here somehow."

SUSAN, LOOKING AT him, whimpered. Her dazed eyes were glistening with tears. "I can't believe that Peter did that!"

"I know how you feel, darling. I'm sorry—horribly sorry."

She seemed to go limp. He caught her into his arms. He had not intended to do that. He had intended to be cautious. But the sight of her destroyed his careful intentions. Holding her almost savagely, he kissed her. Limp in his arms, Susan made no protest—nor did she respond.

Panting, trembling, he put her away from him finally and attempted to cover his mistake "Susan, you must trust me. You know I love you enough to give up my life for you."

Susan looked at him tragically. "I can't believe that Peter—"

"Forget him!" Jason snapped. "He's yellow!"

He went to the door, trying to control his anger. He had been doing that for so many months that now, after his recent hardships, it threatened to blow up.

But her drugged eyes contained neither surprise nor suspicion. Still hungry for the touch of her slim body, he rejected the impulse to return to her. He must be more restrained. He must make her realize what he had suffered to save her. She would, in time, love him. She must love him.

Quietly, he let himself out. He went swiftly down the hall and down the stairs. Crossing the library, he opened a door at the far end of it, and said sharply, "Zarlo! Are you here?"

He did not feel as courageous as his voice sounded, or as he tried to look.

The room he had entered was almost totally dark. High on the side of a wall, a pin-point of light gleamed. Out of the darkness emerged, slowly, the bulk of a figure seated before a table. About eight inches above this table, the pin-point of light was repeated.

Whitelaw knew that Zarlo was occupied with his crystal. He was afraid of Zarlo, of his dark powers.

"Zarlo!" he said sharply.

A DEEP VOICE, crackling as with an electrical discharge, came from the invisible face above the crystal.

"You have failed," the voice said.

Stifling his fear of this man, Whitelaw cried angrily, "That's not true!"

"Your agreement was that you were to bring both of them."

"Was it my fault that the men you sent fumbled their chance? Pennekamp had a gun. I thought they'd overwhelm them. If they'd stayed any longer, the crew would have driven them off, and you wouldn't even have Moore."

He was breathing hard, indignantly. "And you haven't lived up to your agreement. You were to take every precaution that Miss O'Gilvie did not become aware of Moore's being here."

"Is she aware of it?" the crackling voice said.

"She may become aware of it! Why couldn't she have been put in another part of the house?"

The magician said, "Whitelaw, you are a fool. You are a harebrained fool. You will never get away with this. Just what is your plan?"

"Is that schooner waiting on the other side of the island?"

"It is."

"Then my plan is unchanged. I will go through all the motions of rescuing her from here. I will take her through the jungle to the schooner."

"And then—?"

"I will marry her!"

"What a fool you are, Whitelaw! What good will marriage do? She is infatuated with Moore. You can never get him out of her head. Once you reach civilization, she will be through with you."

"No. I'm counting on her gratitude. With Moore dead, she'll turn to me, love me, in time."

"No, Whitelaw. I have seen into her brain. There will never be another man in her brain but Moore. With her wealth, she'll stop at nothing to find out what's become of him."

"How can she find out anything? He will be dead. He left Hong Kong secretly. No one knows how or when or why he left Hong Kong. I told her he went to Japan."

"Yes. You are so infatuated with her beauty, and so greedy to have her money, that you aren't thinking at all. How about the crew of the Buccaneer?"

"They'll be scattered all over the world. You're going to get Pennekamp within a few days. His yacht will go to the nearest port. The crew will disband."

"You're not only a fool, you're a dangerous fool. The Chinese say, 'A man burning with passion follows the undulations of a thought.' You think neither to left nor to right of it. You think of nothing but this girl's body—and her wealth. Don't you realize she will hunt the world for the crew of the Buccaneer? And will find out from them that you lied—that Moore came here?"

"I have it all worked out," Whitelaw said angrily. "We are not going immediately to civilization. We are going to be wrecked conveniently on one of the Javanese Islands, where a ship never calls. A renegade missionary is there—waiting there. I may keep Susan there years—until she falls in love with me."

"I still say you are a harebrained fool! You are exposing me needlessly to danger. I have not yet decided that I will let you carry out your farcical rescue of the young lady. I have taken a fancy to her. I may decide to keep her for myself."

Whitelaw said harshly, "Zarlo, if you go back on our agreement, hell will bust!"

The shapeless figure over the crystal ball chuckled.

7

THE SKULLS

REFUSING TO WEAR dead men's clothes, Peter rummaged about in drawers and presently found a gray flannel shirt and a pair of white duck pants which fitted him fairly well.

He went down the hall, pausing at Whitelaw's door. He knocked, waited, tried the knob. He called softly, but there was no answer. Presuming that the young man from Boston was asleep with exhaustion, Peter proceeded to the staircase, looked up, hesitated, then went down.

He wanted to investigate. He wanted to look for avenues of escape and, generally, to get the lay of the land.

He returned to the hall through which he and Whitelaw had been conducted by the servant. The door at the top of the stone steps, which led down to the great studded entrance door, was locked. To the left of it was another door, closed but not locked. Opening it, Peter discovered another flight of steps, likewise of stone. He walked cautiously down. The steps led to the cellars. In various rooms, quantities of food were stored here, as if for a siege. He wondered where the servants were, the guards. So far he had not seen any one but the butler.

A tunnel ran between rooms and vanished into distant murkiness. He walked down it a hundred feet. It was, possibly, an underground passage to some exit in the jungle. He came to a heavy door which was locked.

He turned about and retraced his steps, climbed the stairs and again entered the hall. He had the feeling that, while he saw no one, he was under constant observation. He entered a spacious drawing room, filled with beautifully carved furniture.

A familiar exotic perfume attracted him. He went to the end of the room and entered a large hall of white stone. It was a kind of reception hall—an immensity of white stone. A fountain, gurgled and splashed in the center of it. This room was at least a hundred and fifty feet square. Along the walls were placed at regular intervals carved chests, the chests, perhaps, of early Spanish explorers. Above them hung great tapestries.

On a small table, he found, with other items, a full box of Japanese safety matches. He thrust the box into a pants pocket.

The room was sickly sweet with the odor of the frangipani blossom. Looking about for the source of the smell, he saw that it emanated from a large stone trough, filled with the waxy white flowers, on a balcony.

Peter climbed a narrow stairway to the balcony, which ran all about the great room. Here were other wall ornaments—actually a museum collection: trophies of all kinds from the southern seas, brilliant old grass tapestries from Tahiti, Papuan lances, spears, bows and arrow, shields, blow-guns, Brunei bronze war gongs. In one corner stood a suit of medieval Japanese armor, reddish-brown.

Peter examined the balcony and its appurtenances with great interest, but was disappointed in what he found.

There was no way of escape. All the windows on the lower floor were heavily barred.

He went to the stone trough. It was a Papuan chieftain's coffin, brilliantly decorated in a savage pattern of reds and greens and blues, resembling the sarcophagus of an Egyptian king. It stood on two pedestals near the edge of the balcony. Peter went close and sniffed the blossoms.

HE WENT TO the rail and looked down. The rail was a thick blue velvet rope, strung along posts, affixed to the top of each post with heavy blue velvet cord. Just below him was a stone table about twelve feet in length. On either end of it stood a Satsuma vase, gold, red, and white. Each of these vases was six or seven feet high.

This great room was, in short, very much like a museum room. Its deathly silence, and the feeling that he was being watched, added to his apprehension. He tried one of the doors near the stone coffin. It opened, to his surprise, into the hall not far from his bedroom.

An idea was tugging at his imagination, but it was not yet ripe. He proceeded down the hall to the stairs again and this time went up. He climbed one flight and found himself on the top floor.

At one end of the hall was a large room of many windows, bright with the early morning sunlight. At the other end was a locked door. A steep flight of steps led to a trapdoor, which, he supposed, opened upon the roof.

He walked into the green room, alert with suspicion and curiosity. The walls were tinted green, the rugs and hangings had been selected to carry out the green color scheme.

This was evidently a game room. There was a billiard table at one end. Here, too, the walls were adorned with trophies of the southern seas—spears, shields, blowguns. In one corner were several glass cases which he did not notice until later, because they were against the glare of the morning sun.

He made a tour about the windows. A door gave upon a balcony. He went out and inspected the scene. Below him the jungle extended in great waves of green in all directions. The horizons consisted of hills. The sea was not visible.

Zarlo, he realized, had constructed this castle with the intention of making it absolutely inaccessible. Certainly, no one would have suspected its existence.

Looking over the edge of the balcony, Peter saw, close to the side of the house, a walled inclosure. The walls, of stone, looked high. Down low on one wall, a large iron ring had been set into the masonry, and from this ring a heavy rusted chain led into a small structure of bamboo and palm thatch built in one corner of the inclosure. He supposed that a large dog was at the other end of the chain, asleep in the thatched structure.

He returned to the green room and for the first time saw the glass cases. There were five of them. Each case was about a foot square, neatly built of plate glass with nickeled metal bindings. Each case stood on a stone pedestal. They looked like exhibition cases in a museum.

He walked swiftly over to them, with his heart suddenly thumping in his throat.

OF THE FIVE cases, the two at the right were empty. Each of the other three contained a human skull!

With fists gripped at his sides, Peter stared at the three grinning death's heads, and felt the color ebbing from his face.

Then he saw that on each case was affixed a neatly lettered placard. He read the first.

Number One
JOHN KYLE
In Memoriam
This gentleman bravely met his death on Soononga Island while chained to a tree in the jungle on the night of August 7, 1927. Leopards, attracted by the smell of rancid meat with which his naked body was smeared, devoured him.

Feeling more than slightly ill, Peter moved to the next case and read the placard.

Number Two
ADAM BRUMPTER
In Memoriam
This gentleman courageously embraced death on Soononga Island while swimming in Shark Cove on the afternoon of October 15, 1929. With hands and feet tied, he was floated out into the cove, supported by corks. Sharks, attracted by the blood flowing from the stump of his severed hand, devoured him.

Shuddering, Peter glanced at the grinning skull. He saw that the top of the skull had been crushed and skillfully repaired with cement Deep gouges in the bone over the left eye socket were probably made by sharks' teeth.

He moved to the next case, revolted yet attracted by a morbid, terrible curiosity. The placard read:

Number Three

HIRAM COOPWOOD

In Memoriam

This gallant gentleman gladly greeted death during the night of May 4, 1932, while staked out on an anthill which housed army ants. The ants, disturbed by his presence, marched out in columns of eight and, fleck by fleck, plucked the skin from his flesh and the flesh from his bones.

Scientific Note: Mr. Coopwood screamed for 48 minutes, before he lapsed into unconsciousness. The last shred of flesh was picked from his skeleton 2 hours and 37 minutes from the time the ants attacked.

Sick with faintness, Peter glanced at the two empty cases. There was a placard on each. Each bore only a name, and, beside the name, a large, neat question mark. Number Four was Roger Pennekamp. Number Five was Peter Moore.

He looked dully at the question mark by his name. He was all but nauseated. What horrible form of death was Zarlo planning for him?

He was conscious of a sensation of shrinking in his flesh, as if every fiber of his body were protesting at the threat of some unimaginably horrible torture.

Panic invaded him. He knew that escape—alive—from this fantastic place was impossible. Yet he could die in his own way, if he wished. He could leap to his death from that balcony. Cornered, it was his only choice—death painlessly rather than by some fiendish prolonged torture. Yet, alive, there was always the slim hope that he might somehow contrive to escape—find Susan and deliver her to safety.

He took a desperate grip on his panic-stricken thoughts.

Zarlo had, of course, reckoned on that—his hoping until the end. Then torture, undoubtedly more hideous than that to which either of these three poor devils had been subjected.

"Wondering?" a crackling voice behind him said.

8

RONGA

PEETER WHEELED ABOUT. Zarlo, tall and dark and sinister, stood there with his arms folded on his chest. In the white satin robe he wore, he gave the effect of great height. His black eyes, set in their darkly blue cavernous sockets, were burning with at light of malignant mirth.

Peter did not, for a moment, see the man standing beside him, a personal guard. A black man, naked except for a loin cloth, staring at Peter with a gummy grin. There was a curved sword, a *parang*, gleaming in the black hand.

In his harsh, deep, crackling voice, Zarlo said, "Mr. Moore, it gives me the greatest pleasure to welcome you to my house. After so many years!" His manner was gravely courteous. "Are you wondering how you will meet your death? Don't wonder, Mr. Moore. Leave that in my hands!"

Peter controlled an impulse to leap on him, but he knew that the grinning black man would have his head split open before he could reach Zarlo's throat.

"We have come a long, long way, Mr. Moore, from the beach at Tuzpan," Zarlo said. His tone was amiable. He was solicitous of Peter's comfort. Did Mr. Moore find things to his liking?

Peter made no answers. He realized that he was the

mouse being toyed with by the cat. His faculties seemed to become sharpened. Every nerve seemed to grow taut, as if preparing for some violent contingency.

"You were examining my pretty skulls. Interesting specimens, aren't they? I think your skull will be a handsome addition to the collection, Mr. Moore."

It was, to Peter, utterly incredible. And his amazement was due, not to Zarlo's grotesque threats, but to the fact that he was not a madman. His mania was only that of revenge—revenge for that old blow to his pride, his vanity and his ambition.

"I want to show you something, Mr. Moore." It was the conversational tone of a genial host, showing a guest through his house.

Peter followed him out onto the balcony. The sun on his face was friendly, warming. He had seen that sun rise in far-away places and under remarkable circumstances. Would he live to see it rise once more?

He went to the end of the balcony. How quickly, how easily he could end this panicky suspense!

From where he stood he could look along the side of the house, down past windows to the roof of the jungle.

Zarlo was talking affably. "Perhaps you are curious about my castle, Mr. Moore. It hasn't always been mine. It's really a fascinating story. It carries out my philosophy of life— dog eat dog. That is the philosophy of all wise men. Take what you want!" He paused, cupped hands to his mouth, and called in a deep, ringing tone:

"Ronga!"

Peter, looking down, saw the heavy chain move. Then a shaggy brown head appeared. A creature looked up. A man, it was! An immense man. His head and face were a mat of tangled brown hair. His body was naked except for a loin cloth. He stared up at the balcony with squinting eyes. His eyes, even at that distance, looked dead.

Peter glanced at Zarlo, who was smiling crookedly.

"Mr. Moore, that man was once the owner of this castle. His name is Fulton D. Agnor. You may have heard of him. He was a New York banker. He grew to hate modern civilization. He had no wife, no family, no relatives, and his friends had betrayed him. He converted his wealth into cash. He looked the world over for a refuge, where he could spend the rest of his life isolated. He found, in this spot, his paradise. At incredible expense he built this castle. When you and your friends drove me out of Tuzpan, I heard of this place. I came. With the power of my will, I drove the soul out of Mr. Fulton D. Agnor, making him the snarling, ravening beast you now see. And I gave him his present name by simply reversing the letters of Agnor—Ronga. A fitting name for such a creature!

"I keep him chained there, an animal. A strange kind of pet, eh? If you should escape from here, I would simply turn Ronga loose."

Peter stared at the thing in the enclosure. Zarlo's voice rose again in that ringing shout: "Ronga! Damn you! Ronga!"

The man-beast, staring up, raised his arms. He snarled.

Zarlo called, "Ronga wants his breakfast. Feed him." And to Peter, "Watch the gate."

A BARRED GATE at the end of the pit opened. A white goat was pushed in by unseen hands. The beast roared. The goat bleated in terror. Ronga rushed, in a great leap, to the end of his chain. The goat danced back beyond his reach, bleating.

The beast rushed again. Peter saw him close his hands, like talons, about the goat's neck. He heard, but did not see, the helpless animal die. Its scream, as its neck was snapped, was like that of a human in agony.

Peter sickened, had looked away. He was filled with loathing, with fury. His senses suddenly cleared. Looking away from the pit, he had glanced down along the wall of the castle. There was a curly brown head protruding from one of the windows, and a small white hand hung limply down over the sill.

It was Susan. She had perhaps seen that bloody affair, and had fainted. Peter saw that her window was on the floor below. He counted the windows from where he stood, estimated where her room was. Just down the hall from his, on the other side!

He glanced quickly at Zarlo. That human monster had not seen. He was staring down with glowing eyes into the pit where the man-beast was savagely devouring the goat.

Jason Whitelaw came out onto the balcony. He was still scowling over his disappointment at the hands of Susan. He glanced at Peter, and his scowl darkened.

Peter stared at him. He had thought that he knew Jason fairly well. And he expected now, not that petulantly scowling young man, but a young man white and quaking with fear.

He expected some kind of signal from Jason, and when the young man scowled at him, as if he did not see him, Peter was puzzled. And his puzzlement became confusion when Jason said, in a surly voice, "Zarlo, what are you going to do with this fellow?"

An unfinished gesture with his thumb indicated Peter. And even then Peter did not comprehend the import of it. It was necessary for him to shift his whole point of view. Jason was an innocent victim of a conspiracy the intention of which was to trap Peter Moore and Roger Pennekamp. At least, Peter had taken that for granted.

His first slow intimation of trouble was the tone with which Jason had addressed Zarlo. It was both petulant and familiar. It clearly indicated, if not a friendship, at least an acquaintance of some standing.

And he realized the shocking truth. Jason had asked Zarlo, in this petulant, familiar tone, what he was going to do with "this fellow"—with him, Peter!

It was hard to grasp all of that at once. Harder still to believe what was a natural, an inevitable conclusion. For a moment, he felt hollow—an "all gone" feeling. Then he was furious. He was murderously furious at this "young man from Boston" who had so heartlessly, so cold-blood-edly betrayed and double crossed him. If it was his last act alive, he would settle that—now!

"You rotten little rat!" he said, and lunged at Whitelaw. His savagely swinging right fist smashed into Whitelaw's jaw. The left fist followed it.

Whitelaw's head snapped up and back. His shoulders swung back. His legs gave way at the knees. He went over and down with a thump.

On his shoulder blades, limp, eyes glassy, he became suddenly invisible. Everything was suddenly invisible.

Something heavy and hard had struck Peter forcibly on the back of his head....

WHEN PETER RECOVERED consciousness he was lying on the bed in his room. Hascomb was seated on the edge of the bed with a whisky bottle in one hand, an empty glass in the other. He still wore his oily grin. He walked over to a table, placed the glass and bottle on it, and returned to the bed.

"In this house," he said, "it is wise to cultivate self-control."

"In any house," Peter dryly amended, and deeply meant it.

His head ached—a painful pulsing behind his eyes. But strength was flowing back into him. His arms and legs tingled. He wanted to get off this bed, but realized the wisdom of utmost caution. He must take it easy. He must think. And when he had thought, he must act.

His plan for his and Susan's escape was ready. But there must be no more mistakes. He must keep his head.

Lying there, with that sneering servant staring at him, he reviewed his plan of action. It must go off smoothly, without a hitch. He fumbled at his pocket, to make sure the box of safety matches was still there. He gripped his hands, to make sure there was ample strength in fists and arms.

And lying there, trying to take it easy, making sure he had overlooked no contingencies which it might lie within his power to anticipate or prevent, he estimated the servant's strength. He must, first of all, put this fellow out of commission.

Hascomb was, obviously, suspicious of him. Obviously, he had been stationed here as a guard. He looked and acted as if he were prepared for trouble. His eyes did not once shift from Peter's eyes. He was clever. He knew that when a man plans trouble, his eyes give the signal. And if Peter's eyes gave the signal, Hascomb would act before he could act.

Peter lowered his lids as if he were sleepy. Hascomb sat down again, still staring at him. Peter waited. Seeming to drowse, he watched Hascomb's eyes. Perhaps five minutes passed. Then Hascomb's eyes, tiring, perhaps, of Peter's face, went for a moment to the window.

Peter seized that chance. He sat up suddenly, threw his right arm about Hascomb's neck and held it in a hammer-lock.

Hascomb leaped up, pulling Peter with him, as Peter had hoped he would. The servant tried to kick Peter in the shins, but Peter had anticipated that, too.

Peter slugged him twice, once with each fist, and Hascomb's interest in conflict evaporated. He sagged, a dead weight, in Peter's arms.

Peter laid him on the bed and strode to the door. He was now going to execute his difficult and dangerous program. There must be no hitch, there must be no hesitation.

At the door, with his hand on the knob, he took a deep breath. He let himself out, ran to the door down the hall which gave upon the balcony of the great white stone room, and fell swiftly to work. He took down a magnificent battle-ax from its bronze hooks, and quickly chopped the cords which bound the thick velvet rope, serving as a balcony rail, to the posts. He chopped through the rope at each end. Then he coiled up approximately one hundred feet of the rope and threw the coil down near the Papuan coffin.

He now snatched a stout Marquesan lance from the wall and addressed himself to the coffin. He hated to destroy such a beautiful specimen, but it was necessary to his plans. He was, so to speak, working in the dark. He did not know what his enemies' plans were, and he was working on the theory that fire is best fought with fire, surprises with surprises.

IT TOOK ALL his strength to move the handsome stone coffin, with its sickly smelling blossoms, but he did move it. He moved it a fraction of an inch, with the lance as a lever. Another fraction. Another. As it toppled, he put his shoulder against it, and gave a herculean shove.

The coffin began to fall. Peter snatched up the coil of velvet rope in one hand, the battle-ax in the other, and went to the door. He waited just long enough to be sure the job was done. With a lurch, the coffin fell.

Peter opened the door, ran into the hall and to the door which he believed was Susan's. Pressing his mouth into the corner formed by door and jamb, he called her name.

And at that instant, the castle of Zarlo was filled with a roaring, as of a mighty explosion. Even Peter, who had caused that terrific din, was surprised by the volume, the intensity of it. It sounded as if a charge of dynamite had gone off.

The Papuan coffin, weighing upwards of a ton, had toppled over the balcony; had fallen with a mighty impact on the twelve-foot stone table below, shattering it. The two enormous Satsuma vases, one at either end of the table, had joined in the tumult. Each had fallen to the marble floor, a second apart, and to the mighty echoing reverberations of the falling coffin were added the new crashing as the uproar of the smashing vases was added to the wild tumult. It was terrific.

And it worked. Surprise fought surprise. There were shouts, hoarse cries from all directions as men from all over the house surged to the scene of demolition.

And Peter, with the battle-ax, was chopping through a door. When the door gave, he ran inside and propped the battle-ax under the knob to prevent invasion.

Susan, with frantic arms about his neck, was sobbing, "Peter! Darling!"

She began babbling questions. Peter was too busy to answer. He seized a long bench and dragged it to the window, making sure that the ends considerably over-lapped the window. About the middle of this he knotted one end of the velvet rope.

Men were hammering at the door. Peter climbed over the sill, grasped the rope in both hands, told Susan to hang to his neck.

When she was hanging there, he started sliding down. The velvet rope burned through his hands.

Then he discovered that he was, so to speak, midway between the frying pan and the fire. Above him a black hand containing a knife began to hack at the rope. Below him was the pit containing the man-beast, looking up at them, with claws distended.

Peter, making his plans an inch at a time, slid down faster. When he was dangling just above the pit, he braced his feet against the wall and pushed with all his strength. He and Susan swung out. When they were poised, for a breathless moment, beyond the outer wall of the pit, he let go, just as the knife at the window above cut through the rope.

They fell perhaps a dozen feet into a thick tangle of bushes, starred with bright red small flowers. Peter would remember those flowers. Like innumerable little red stars, they welcomed him and Susan.

Susan screamed and Peter had suddenly the sensation of being stabbed in a million places. The bushes cushioned their fall. But the bushes stabbed and raked them with thorns.

With the breath almost knocked out of him, Peter pushed through the thorns, dragging Susan after him by the hand, toward a path. Down this path they ran. It presently joined the jungle trail up which Peter and Whitelaw and the red-headed man had come a few hours previously.

They would, of course, be followed. He had anticipated that, but he had planned, with the confusion resulting from the crashing of the coffin, to gain a few precious seconds. Granted those seconds, he had another plan to insure their escape.

Still running, they reached the end of the jungle path which then entered the high, parched cactus grass. And behind them, as they ran, they heard the snarling roar of Ronga.

Zarlo had threatened that. Evidently, he had acted immediately on the sounding of the alarm, had turned the man-beast loose.

Peter, looking back, from the middle of the great field of tall grass, saw the waving of it as the beast entered the field behind them.

HE TOLD SUSAN to run on to the end of the field. Then he extracted the box of Japanese safety matches from his pocket and began swiftly to ignite them and toss them behind him as he followed her. He threw flaming matches to left and right.

The cactus grass burned swiftly. Wherever a flaming match fell, it ignited, and the flames fiercely spread. As Peter ran to overtake Susan, flames roared behind him. Already, black smoke was gushing up from the highly inflammable grass, and so swiftly did the fire spread that Peter was himself in danger of being trapped.

He ran for it. At the edge of the jungle he paused beside Susan and looked back. In all directions the fire he had started was spreading. Dense black smoke, shot with leaping flame, gushed and roared upward. And above this uproar he could hear the roaring of the beast, frustrated, driven back and back by the flames.

Peter was laughing with relief and elation. His whole plan of action had carried through without a hitch. The explosive crash of the coffin and the two great vases had sufficiently demoralized the household for him to get Susan safely away. And the firing of the cactus grass would withhold pursuit, would give Susan and him at least a half hour's head start.

"We're safe!" he exulted. "Now we've got to travel fast."

The rest of the way was, he believed, comparatively simple. The trek back to the river. The only possible contingency was that the boat might be guarded. He did not believe it would be guarded. Certainly, the redhead would have been too exhausted from the trip to return and guard it.

But Peter was not worrying about that. Luck had so far been with him. And luck, once it began to smile, had a way of continuing to smile.

Yet his plans were wrecked by a source from which he would have least expected it. Susan! Susan was tired. Susan was dazed. Stimulated for a time by the excitement of their getaway, she was now suffering a kind of relapse.

A hundred yards beyond the edge of the burning field, she declared she could go no farther. She felt dizzy, sick, strange. Peter offered to carry her.

She cried, "Don't touch me! Keep away from me!"

He said, incredulously, "Good Lord, what's the matter?"

"You don't understand! Keep away from me!"

He stopped and stared at her, with fists planted on hips. He said impatiently, "Stop this nonsense. We've got away to a fine start. We're going to push on. Come on!"

"No, no! I can't go with you."

He was now thoroughly perplexed. "What's the matter? What's got into you?"

She shrank away from him, took a few steps back toward the castle. "I can't go! I've got to go back! He's ordering me to go back. He's willing me! I can't stop him. I've got to go!"

Before Peter could prevent her, she had started to run back down the path toward the smoking field.

He shouted to her to stop. She ran like a deer. He was too astonished for a moment to move. What she had said had fairly paralyzed his muscles.

Then, realizing, he started after her. By the time he had reached the field she had vanished. He shouted at the top of his lungs. And ran harder, into the smoke.

A root tripped him. He fell, sprawling upon the embers of smoldering roots.

He dragged himself wearily to his feet. He could not catch her now. She had gone back to the castle. Bitterly, he started walking through the smoke. His plan of escape had worked perfectly—every detail had worked so perfectly! He felt sick with disappointment. And he appreciated, as he had never done before, the diabolical cleverness of Zarlo.

9

END OF A FOOL

WHEN SUSAN REACHED the castle, the bronze-studded door was open. She ran fairly into the arms of a half-dozen black men, all armed with knives, who were starting out.

They took her to Zarlo, in his study. Looking at her with expressionless eyes, he ordered them to lock her in the room next to her old room. His voice was lazy, but he looked dangerous.

Susan, locked in this room, came partially to her senses. In stark terror she realized what she had done. Fighting down an impulse to scream, she seated herself on the edge of the bed and tried to compose herself. She was seated there, twisting her hands in her lap, softly whimpering, when Jason Whitelaw came in. His face was white and grim. There was a dark, raw bruise on his chin from the blow Peter had given him on the balcony, and there was ugliness in his eyes.

Closing the door, he advanced on her. He said thickly, "Susan, you've got to listen to me. I love you. I'm going to get you out of this."

Susan, utterly unnerved, sprang up. She struck him in the face with her fist. They were futile blows, but they accomplished one object. They caused Whitelaw to drop the key. He forgot the key. He forgot caution, too. He forgot how careful he was going to be.

He caught Susan in his arms, held her so tightly that she could not move. He began hungrily to kiss her. He kissed her mouth, her throat.

Susan realized, perhaps for the first time, just what his intentions were. And the realization transformed her into a young human wildcat. She twisted out of his arms. She doubled up her small fists and threw herself at him.

Whitelaw, surprised by the very fury of her attack, gave ground. They were not far from the open door now. And before the savagery of her attack, he backed away until he was in the hall.

And before he could prevent her, she had slammed the door and dragged a chair under the knob. She was, for the moment, safe. But only, she realized, for the moment.

She understood perfectly the thorough perfidy of Jason Whitelaw. He would, she knew, stop at nothing now.

And he proved this by his immediate actions. Recovering from the fury of that attack, faced by the shut door, Whitelaw lost all hold on his self-restraint. He battered at the door with his fists. He shouted. He implored, he entreated, he threatened.

The door remained closed. He kicked at it, and again he hammered on it. He shouted until he was hoarse.

Backed into a corner, white with terror, Susan listened.

In a frenzy of frustration, the disappointed lover kicked and beat at the door until his fists and feet were throbbing with pain.

There was another way! He would get into that room! He ran into the room adjoining—the room Susan had previously occupied. There was a cornice about eight inches in length which ran along the outside wall. He would enter the room in which she was now barricaded by means of this cornice!

Only a man half mad with fury would have considered such a dangerous route.

Zarlo's jeering criticism of him occurred to him as he started along the cornice: "A man burning with passion follows the undulations of a thought. You are a hare-brained fool!"

Susan was at the open window and heard his harsh breathing, and the scuffle of his shoes on that narrow ledge of stone. She tried frantically to close the window, but it was jammed and would not move.

Sobbing, she thought, "I'll push him off! I'll kill him!"

Below her, as she glanced down, she saw the beast. He had evidently been returned to his inclosure by Zarlo. The hair of his face and head was singed. He lifted his hairy arms and snarled.

She looked back at Whitelaw, and tried again to pull the window down.

Then she heard Whitelaw yell. She looked out in time to see him clawing desperately at the smooth wall above him, to see him lose his balance and plunge downward.

And she saw the beast lift his arms to catch Whitelaw. Her heart seemed to stop. Whitelaw was plunging down toward those hairy upraised arms.

The beast uttered a snarling roar as Whitelaw fell into his powerful arms. Whitelaw had been saved from a dreadful death for a fate even more dreadful.

As Susan stared, Whitelaw screamed out in agony. The

beast was crushing, tearing him to death! Through a mist
of faintness, Susan heard the snapping of bones. Then the
beast picked up the broken carcass in his arms and hurled
it against a wall.

Then Zarlo leaped into the inclosure and the beast
became quiet.

A HAMMERING AT her door distracted Susan. She heard
Peter's voice and she ran to open it. As she unlocked and
opened the door, another man plunged down the hall—a
red-headed man.

Susan screamed a warning. As Peter came into the room,
she tried to shut the door, but the red-headed man had
wedged his foot in the crack. Before Peter could help her,
the door smashed open and the redhead charged in with
automatic pistol drawn.

But Peter had a chair ready, in his hands. He brought the
chair swinging down on the charging redhead. He dropped
the pistol, but he came right on. Peter lifted the chair again
for another swing, but the redhead came in under it, and
grabbed his throat in powerful fingers.

Peter dropped the chair. His breath was cut off. Susan's
screams seemed to come from far away.

In a twisting lunge, he carried the redhead to the floor.
For just a moment, the fingers at his throat slipped away.
And Peter drove his fists like battering rams into the
distorted face. In a space of seconds he struck a dozen
tremendous blows before the redheaded man could reach
his throat again.

The fingers relaxed, fell limply at the ends of limp arms.

Peter picked up the pistol and staggered to the door,
which Susan had closed.

He said hoarsely, "Come on. It's our last chance!" And flung the door open.

The hall outside was, at a glance, a solid, packed mass of black bodies, black men waiting.

Peter fired into them. A man fell. Another. He aimed deliberately. They fell back, turned to rush him, but they wilted before that deadly fire. Some ran. Peter dropped the pistol when the hammer fell, finally, with a click, and picked up a *parang*. With this, he ran one black man through the throat.

Those who remained were too terrified to touch him. He took Susan's hand and ran with her down the hall to the stairs. And down the stairs.

And at the bottom of the stairs Zarlo and the beast were waiting!

Black men, recovered from their terror at his savage counter-attack, were following Peter and Susan down the stairs. Except for the *parang*, he was unarmed. And against such odds he was helpless.

Zarlo, standing with his arms folded across his chest, said in his crackling voice, "Ronga! Get him! Kill him! Kill the girl!"

And Ronga started up the stairs toward him, with glittering bloodshot eyes.

Peter was, for a moment, unable to move. The beast was like some horrible apparition. The singed hair of his head and face was matted, dripping with blood—Whitelaw's blood. His hands and arms to the shoulders were red and gleaming with the wet blood. His chest was slimy with gore.

"Get him, Ronga!" Zarlo cried ringingly.

The beast snarled. Susan screamed. She backed against the wall and screamed again and again.

PETER, KNOWING THE superhuman strength of those bloody arms, lifted the *parang* and leaped. He was eight or ten steps above Ronga when he leaped. His intention was to strike the blade into the beast's throat.

But Ronga anticipated that. The blade snapped out of Peter's hand as the beast's paw flicked up and clamped down on his wrist. With a snarling roar, he grabbed Peter against his chest.

But before he could encircle him with the other arm, Peter struck with his left fist with every ounce of power he possessed. And there was science behind that blow.

It might have killed an ordinary man. It shocked and dazed Ronga only for a moment. But that moment gave Peter an advantage. It gave him the chance to free his other hand, and this too, he sent swiftly and savagely into action.

He slugged Ronga in the jaw a second time, and followed with another sledge hammer blow from his left.

Zarlo was calling upon Ronga to kill him.

The beast was backing down the stairs. He seemed to sag. The bloodshot eyes were swimming.

"Go back there!" Zarlo thundered. "Get him! Kill him, I tell you!"

Ronga, with a muttered groan, collapsed at Zarlo's feet.

Peter ran back up the stairs. He grasped Susan's hand and pulled her down into the hall.

Before Zarlo could prevent him he had pulled Susan past and to the other end of the hall. The door leading into the small hall was locked. The door adjoining it was a few inches ajar.

There remained only one possible avenue of escape—the cellars!

Peter yanked open that door and half carried Susan down the long flight of stairs. He felt utterly exhausted. His legs would hardly support him. His breath was like fire in his lungs. Only the vital necessity of prompt, swift action sustained him.

Susan, sobbing, gasping, cried:

"What are we going to do?"

He answered wearily:

"There may be an underground passage. If there isn't, we're done for."

They reached the door of the tunnel. Peter searched for a tool; found a sledgehammer in a near-by room. He swung it down on the lock. His arms ached so that he could hardly stand the pain of lifting the sledgehammer, bringing it down. The cellar seemed to fill with a mist. He blinked sweat out of his eyes and swung and swung. Almost senseless with exhaustion, it seemed to him that all of his life he had been swinging the sledgehammer at this obstinate lock.

But the lock presently disintegrated. Peter dropped the sledgehammer, and with the little strength that remained, opened the door.

Beyond was an empty room, approximately twelve feet square. No doors led from it. It was comprised of solid walls of masonry.

"RONGA!" ZARLO CRIED. "Get up! Damn you, get up! Get after them!"

He kicked the recumbent figure in the ribs.

The beast shuddered. He rolled slowly over onto his back

and sat up. He looked up at Zarlo with strange eyes. He bent forward until he was crouched on his haunches, and his eyes stared and stared at Zarlo.

"Damn you! Get up!"

The beast slowly got up, pushing himself up as a gorilla might. He stood a moment, swaying, still staring at Zarlo, never, in fact, for an instant taking his eyes from Zarlo.

And Zarlo grew alarmed. Once again he shouted, "Ronga! Damn you, follow them! Get them! Get that man! I want them killed—both of them!"

Ronga shook his head slightly, in the gesture of one dazed. Swiftly he reached out and pinioned Zarlo's arms to his sides.

Zarlo cried sharply for help. But there was no help. The black men had fled. The castle echoed emptily to his cries. With a savage lunge he broke away from the beast and started up the stairs, a few steps at a time, backing up, shouting.

And step by step Ronga followed him.

Halfway up, Zarlo ran to the top of the stairs, and the beast, agile as an orang-utan, followed. Still shouting, Zarlo ran up the next flight of stairs and into the green room, the beast only a few feet behind him, deathly silent, menacingly alert.

"Go back!" Zarlo shouted.

The beast followed him, eyes staring, until Zarlo backed against the glass cases containing the skulls of his three victims. He stepped aside. The beast, swinging his arms, swept the cases from their pedestals. Glass crashed. Three skulls rolled onto the floor.

The beast picked up the nearest. He hurled it at Zarlo.

The skull missed, crashed through a window. He picked up another, and hurled it. Zarlo yelped with pain as it cracked his elbow. He picked up the skull as it fell and savagely threw it back at Ronga.

Ronga warded it off with the palm of one hand. He kicked the third skull aside with his naked foot. Then he sprang on Zarlo. Once again he pinioned his arms to his sides. He lifted him easily over his head.

The master magician kicked and yelled and struggled. The beast, carrying him, walked to the balcony door and kicked it open.

Zarlo, realizing his intention, began to implore.

"Ronga! Put me down! I will give you anything! Ronga, listen! I will set you free! I will go! This place will be yours again! Ronga! Good God—"

It ended in a shriek of agonized terror. Ronga had stopped at the railing.

Sounds of his terror, not intelligible words, flowed, in a thick, shrill stream from the lips of the master magician.

Ronga cast him down carelessly, as though he were casting away something utterly worthless. And he watched until the falling man struck the wall of the inclosure and rebounded, a shapeless thing in a white robe, to lie across the heavy iron chain.

10

THE BEAST

IN THE SMALL cellar room into which Peter's optimism
had led him, Susan was bandaging the wound in Peter's
arm. He had not known he was stabbed there.

He was sitting on the floor with his back, in more senses
than one, against the wall. His head had sagged down onto
his chest. The loss of so much blood had done for him. He
had not the strength to stand.

And Susan was whimpering her contriteness. She had
been impelled, against her will, to return to the castle. Zarlo
had willed her to return.

A sound of heavy, harsh breathing arrested her apol-
ogy. Some one was coming down the tunnel toward them.
Susan could not see who it was. A short flight of steps
intervened. And suddenly she screamed, thinly.

"Peter!" she gasped. She was frantically squeezing his
hand. "Look! What will we do?"

A shadow, cast by one of the electric bulbs in the arched
ceiling of the tunnel, came toward them. A head—shoulders. A long, black, sinister shadow.

"The beast!" Susan screamed.

She cowered down against Peter. The beast came slowly
toward them. They could hear his bare feet, his heels, softly

thudding on the stone, in a measured beat. It was like the approach of an automaton.

Peter tried to rise. There was no strength left in him. He tried twice. The third time he came weakly, swaying, to his feet. But if his back had not been against the wall, he would have collapsed.

Slowly the beast walked down the steps. Susan, clinging to Peter, shuddered as his feet, then his legs, appeared.

Peter drew a deep breath. The sledgehammer was lying near the door, where it had slipped out of his limp hands.

He could support himself, he believed, but he knew he could not reach the sledgehammer in time. Once again mist seemed to be rising about him.

Then it was too late. The beast entered the room. He looked at them, from one white face to the other.

He said quietly, in a voice of unutterable weariness, "Don't be alarmed. Please don't be alarmed. There has been some terrific confusion—like a horrible nightmare. I don't know what has happened. I—I wish you'd help me to understand. My name is Fulton Agnor. This is supposed to be my house, yet something has happened. I wonder— would you be so good—would you explain?"

Peter, in that swimming mist, felt strength return with hope restored. He heard Susan laugh with hysterical relief. Fulton Agnor's soul had been restored to him when Zarlo plunged to his death. That, at least, was Susan's emphatic explanation, and she would listen to no other.

THEY RETURNED THAT evening, Peter on a stretcher, to the river and the speedboat, and at dusk they boarded the Buccaneer. Fulton Agnor had proved to be a solicitous host. He had urged them to remain, and Susan had wanted to remain, but Peter, perhaps, did not put too much faith in Mr. Agnor's sanity.

Roger Pennekamp met them as they came up the ship's ladder, a haggard man, aged by worry. Peter's first question was, "What have you done with Tackaberry?"

"I did what you said. He is in irons."

Later, refreshed by a bath, a shave, clean clothes and a stiff drink of excellent Bourbon, Peter joined Mr. Pennekamp and Susan on deck. The yacht was slipping through moonlit jade water and the headland of Skull Island was fading astern.

Susan had been relating the day's excitement to Mr. Pennekamp. She was already seeing her experience as a thrilling, a "perfectly fascinating" adventure.

Peter seated himself on the wicker settee beside her, and Susan snuggled against him and looked into his face with shining eyes. He wondered if her appetite for adventurous thrills would ever be satisfied. Evidently not. Her attitude—and he was convinced of its sincerity—was that she would, by tomorrow morning, be delighted to embark on another adventure, if a sufficiently thrilling adventure should happen along. And he was tired of adventuring. And the thought of marrying Susan became, once again, too dismaying to contemplate.

She cuddled her warm little hand into his and sighed. Then she asked how Mr. Pennekamp and Peter had found their way to Zarlo's hideout.

"A crystal ball," Peter said dryly. "That night in Hong Kong we saw the headland of Skull Island in the crystal ball—and I recognized it."

She straightened up and said triumphantly:

"There! And you won't believe in occult demonstrations!"

"Not in that one," Peter said, and grinned. "The day after we'd seen it, I investigated the crystal. I found a pair of fine wires leading from the taboret, down through the deck and eventually into Captain Tackaberry's room. Under the crystal was a clever little arrangement—a small electric bulb, a lens, and a beautifully hand-colored transparency—a tiny colored film of the headland.

"When the skipper knew that Mr. Pennekamp or anybody else wanted to see an image in the ball, the skipper generously obliged. In his cabin, he turned on current through a rheostat, so that the image, at first dim and weak, became clearer and brighter. And, when the demonstration was over, smoothly faded out.

"Knowing then that Tackaberry was a tool of Zarlo's I would have had him put in irons immediately. But I wanted to see him play his game out. I wanted to go to Skull Island, because I believed you were there."

"You're wonderful!" Susan marveled.

"No," he said. "Dumb. Very dumb. I waited too long. I didn't expect that surprise attack so soon."

The look she gave him was a curious mixture of admiration and defiance.

"I don't care," she complained. "There is something in such things. Zarlo had Mr. Agnor and me completely under the control of his will."

"With the aid of drugs," Peter said. "And post-hypnotic suggestion. He kept Mr. Agnor drugged—therefore soulless, for six years—a slave to his will. I still maintain that occultism, mysticism, is the bunk."

A protesting murmur from Mr. Pennekamp indicated

that the oil millionaire's faith in occultism was by no means shaken. And Susan's mouth was already open, to protest and argue.

"Zarlo," Peter said, "had a remarkable magnetic personality."

"How," Susan cried, "did he make me return? He did! I know he did!"

"He had drugged you," Peter argued. "While you were drugged, he easily hypnotized you. I grant that. He planted ideas—orders—in your head. One idea was that, in case you tried to escape, you were to return."

"Is that what you mean by posthypnotic suggestion?"

"Yep."

"And you say that that is why I returned to the castle?"

Peter grinned. "That's right, Susan."

"Then I think it's perfectly ridiculous. I absolutely believe I was enslaved by that monster's will. I absolutely believe in all sorts of occultism! And I think it's perfectly fascinating!"